Also by Richard Bach

Stranger to the Ground
Biplane
Nothing by Chance
Jonathan Livingston Seagull
A Gift of Wings
Illusions
There's No Such Place as Far Away
The Bridge Across Forever
One
Running from Safety
Out of My Mind
Rescue Ferrets at Sea
Air Ferrets Aloft
Writer Ferrets: Chasing the Muse

RICHARD BACH

THE FERRET CHRONICLES

Illustrated by the Author

Ferret House Press

Rancher Ferrets on the Range

SCRIBNER

NEW YORK LONDON TORONTO SYDNEY SINGAPORE

SCRIBNER
1230 Avenue of the Americas
New York, NY 10020

SCRIBNER and design are trademarks of Macmillan Library Reference USA, Inc.,
used under license by Simon & Schuster, the publisher of this work.

For information regarding special discounts for bulk purchases,
please contact Simon & Schuster Special Sales at 1-800-456-6798
or business@simonandschuster.com

Text set in Fry's Baskerville

Manufactured in the United States of America

1   3   5   7   9   10   8   6   4   2

Library of Congress Cataloging-in-Publication Data

Bach, Richard.
Rancher ferrets on the range/Richard Bach
p. cm.—(The ferret chronicles)
1. Ferrets—Fiction. 2. Ranch life—Fiction. I. Title.

PS3552.A255 R36 2003
813'.54—dc21
2002030999

ISBN 0-7432-2755-7

Rancher Ferrets on the Range

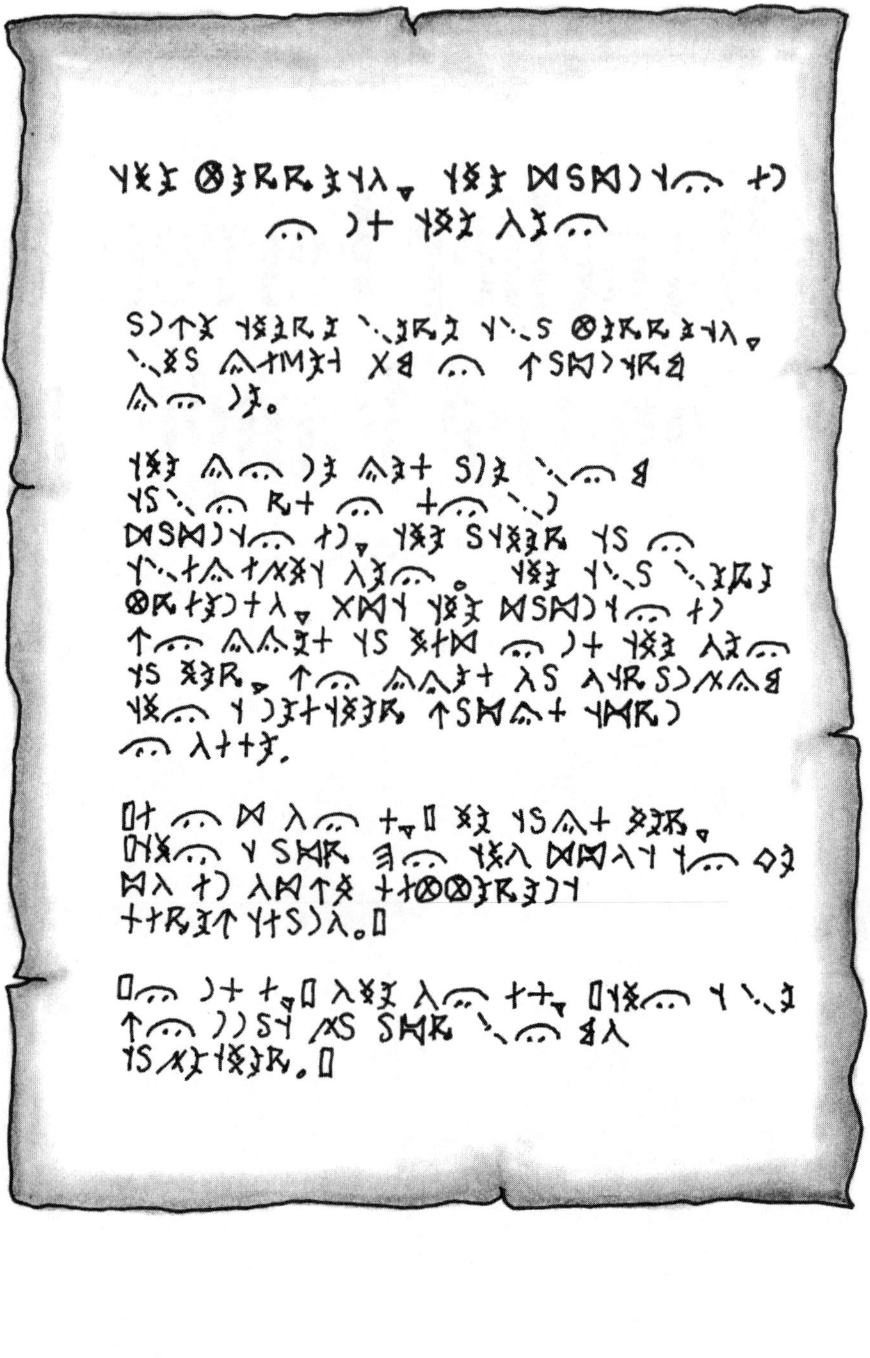

The Ferrets, the Mountain and the Sea

Once there were two ferrets who lived by a country lane.

The lane led one way toward a dawn mountain, the other to a twilight sea. The two were friends, but the mountain called to him and the sea to her, called so strongly that neither could turn aside.

"I am sad," he told her, "that our paths must take us in such different directions."

"And I," she said, "that we cannot go our ways together."

The two held their love warmly in their hearts, but listened to their highest right and walked the lane toward its opposite ends.

After many adventures, they discovered that the path toward the dawn led over the mountain to the sea, and the path toward the twilight led across the sea to the mountain.

On the other side of the mountain, on the other side of the sea, the lovers met again, and their paths were one.

Our highest right knows all futures. As we listen to its whisper, we find that the prize ahead is our own greatest happiness.

—Antonius Ferret, *Fables*

CHAPTER 1

"I never saw a ranchpaw ever wore a *blue* hat . . ."

She was just a kit, and truth to tell so was he, when he taught the silver-fur Cheyenne Jasmine Ferret to ride delphins.

She adjusted the sky-color brim lower over her eyes, hint of a smile. "I'm not a ranchpaw, Montgomery Ferret, and it'll do you well to remember that. You teach me everything you know, please, and leave my hat out of it!"

They lived near the end of the river road, their parents' ranches side by side, sheltered from the west by the lofty Sweetroot Mountains, from the north and east by wide Montana wilderness. Before school and after, before chores and after, they rode together.

Now Monty Ferret sat relaxed upon Boffin, his gray delphin, paws crossed easily atop the animal's mane, and watched his lovely friend. "When you're asking her to jump, you want to get your weight back, Cheye, you want to shift your weight off your front paws, let Starlet get her head up to jump."

"She doesn't want to jump, Monty." Cheyenne cantered the delphin to her friend, slowed to a walk close by, a tight circle around the unruffled Boffin. "I move back and she still doesn't want to jump. She stops."

"So what do you think is wrong?"

"She doesn't want to jump."

"If that doesn't beat everything," said her instructor. "She wants to jump when I ride her. Why is that, do you suppose?"

"She likes you. All the delphins like you." The kit burst with frustration. "She doesn't want to jump because I'm not *you*!"

"Now you're stubborn again, and that's likely not going to be much help," said Monty, a picture of calm. "So let me ask again. What's she *thinking*? Ever you find an animal does something you don't understand, ask yourself: *What's it thinking?*"

Contrite, determined to learn: "How?"

"Go into her mind! Pretend you're Starlet right now. Now you're coming round the turn, you see the fence, you're thinking *I want to jump, for Cheyenne!* Why don't you do it?"

A long silence, his student nearly in a trance, imagining. "I can't jump."

"Good. Why can't you jump?"

The kit considered, her mind in the delphin's, all at once realizing. *"I'm not running fast enough! Cheyenne's holding me back!"*

Her teacher smiled. "Now that's interesting, isn't it? Do you think that's true? Are you going to try that jump again?"

Her fur a radiant fall of light, her head low over the delphin's mane, pastel hat barely showing above Starlet's ears, Cheyenne wheeled without a word, urged her mount topspeed around the turn toward the jump. Drumbeat

3

hooves pounded from the earth, echoed from stone-canyon walls. Sand kicked into the air behind the two, pebbles flying.

Monty watched. "Go, Cheye," he murmured.

The silver kit lifted her weight, whispered to her delphin, "*Fly!*"

A flick of Starlet's tail, the two launched into silence, slow-motion airborne on the wind, no hoofbeats for a long pause, the low fence rail blurring beneath them.

Then ground thudded and trembled, the echoes again, Starlet swerving at the touch of Cheyenne's paw, cutting a half-circle to stop, breathing hard, by Monty and Boffin.

The kit's eyes sparkled. "It works!"

Her burly little trainer nodded.

"What did I do?" She was breathless with excitement and victory.

He said nothing. Tilted his head, listened.

"I was in her mind! I wanted to jump . . . *she* wanted to jump!"

"I reckon so."

"Again?"

"Does she want to jump again, Cheye, or does she want to rest, now?"

The delphin's ears tilted ahead, she shook the wind from her mane.

Cheyenne flashed a smile, eyes darker than midnight. "She wants to jump!"

"You show her how . . ."

Then his friend was off again at a gallop.

Montgomery Ferret practiced watching with his ears, with his body, eyes closed. Out near the border-fence, here comes the turn. He felt the hoofbeats. A little slow.

Cheyenne urged her delphin one beat faster toward the fence, shifted her weight and called the animal into the air. Silence . . . two . . . three . . . hoofbeats pounding again, slowing, turning.

Finally Monty could stand it no more. He leaned forward, whispered, "Let's show 'em, Boffers. The high fence, now . . ."

The kits were ever together, Monty and Cheyenne growing up inseparable: out riding, exploring, noses in field guides about wild plants and animals and stars in the sky. From time to time, the two would excuse themselves from table, ask to be off for a sunrise ride before one family or the other had finished breakfast. "Your juice, at least," parents would say.

Monty's brother Zander watched and said it for them all: "Born for each other, those two. Different as rock and water, alike as birds on a branch!"

Cousin Jupe had looked up at this, nodded *well said*. Everyone knew, he thought, no one noticed.

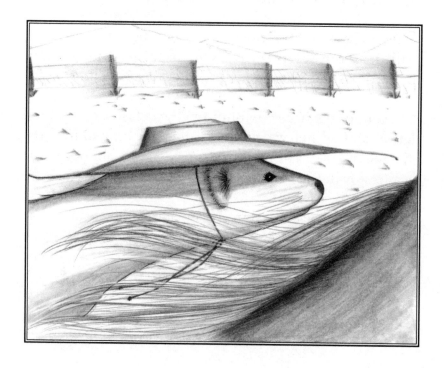

Monty's gift with animals he vowed to pass along to his friend, and nearly did. Yet while butterflies would land at once upon his upturned paw, they flew cautious near Cheyenne, waiting a more formal invitation.

I'm not as gentle as Monty, she thought, I'm not as peaceful, inside.

He taught her patience, sprinkling seeds on the wide brim of that powder-blue hat, bid her stand motionless till the chickadees came to breakfast. Patience she learned, and the delight of their tiny weight, trusting, on the edge.

She considered that, and told him, one day. "I trust you with my life," she said, the two and their delphins far up Sable Canyon. "I never thought about it, but all of a sudden, Monty, it's always been true." She said the words as though she had never thought them before. *"I trust you."*

He nodded, matter-of-fact. "I'll be here for you, Cheye. Long as I live. No matter what."

If the world outdoors was Monty's first love, the world indoors, of images on-screen, was Cheyenne's. Weekends, after they explored the countryside, the two ferrets rode to Little Paw and the gilt-and-scarlet middle-row seats at CineMustelid.

"This one you will love, kitlets." Alexopoulos Ferret passed torn ticket stubs back through the window of his last-century box office, shipped board by gilded board across the sea from the island of Chios. "He is a young director, this Heshsty Ferret, but watch what he does with the light, the way he lets the light tell his story!"

Soon Cheyenne inquired of Alexopoulos whether she might help at the theater, sell tickets and popcorn, change posters and marquee, clean and polish—anything to find how magic projects to the heart from images on-screen.

"I can pay only a little," he said, "but the movies will be free."

Every showing of every film, Cheyenne Ferret learned. The more she cared, the more she noticed the power of the slightest motion, how actors can show a story's crisis, close up, as simply as shifting their thought behind an unchanging expression.

Alexopoulos answered her questions, tested her with questions of his own, filled her with the lore of film. He watched her closely, saw a quality grow about her, in time, that made other animals turn their heads to see.

Only in part is it her beauty that attracts them, he thought. It is more than beauty. Cheyenne Ferret has a certain . . . she has a transparency to others. He nodded, for that was it. Within herself lay the magic that she felt from the screen.

8

Times the lessons she set were hard, to act every scene without a sound, standing alone in the dark at the back of the theater. One matinee, missing a line for the third time, she whispered despair as he passed, "I'll never learn it, Mr. Alexopoulos!"

"Probably not," he whispered back. "It takes a great heart, this work."

With Monty she would watch each film through yet again, her eyes on his face more than the screen. How does this scene touch him? Can I sense what he feels?

Actors move their spirit into fiction's mind, she thought, as Monty moves his into delphins'. In film, spirit and technique need each other. Should either fail, a story is lost, an audience unchanged.

Time and again tears streaked her fur as the friends emerged from the dark, untied their delphins and rode home together.

"It's so beautiful, Monty!" she told him once, riding home from *Desperate Voyage*. "Laura Ferret loved him all along, didn't she? And she never told him till the end! All that time, and poor Stefan never knew."

"Beats me why she didn't tell him up front!" He lifted his hat, ran a paw to smooth his fur. "If I would've been her, I would've told him. He still could make his choice, he'd just have had more information to work with if he knew, seems to me."

"No, you silly!" Cheyenne leaned toward her friend in the sunset, Starlet and Boffin side by side. *"I couldn't tell you, Stefan. I wanted, but I couldn't. Love isn't love, when it's asked . . ."*

The way she said the words they came softer, more intimate than they had from the screen itself. It was as though she were speaking not to some distant Stefan but to Montgomery Ferret, close enough to touch.

Instead of fading as she learned, her fascination with the pictures grew. An actor can let us share a life, she saw, let us *live* a life that we could never touch, otherwise. An actor can show what it is to make different decisions, become a wiser, deeper animal. How would it feel, she wondered, to give such a gift?

She thought about this for a long time, the friends talked, and one day she decided.

"I'm going to Hollywood," she told him, their picnic spread on red-check gingham, crisp wild plants they had gathered: greens, nuts, berries. A canteen of mountain water hung from a pine branch nearby. In the grass about them drifts of pale blue mountain daisies listened, nodded agreement.

Monty was silent. It has to be, he thought, and that's all right. She's studied hard, she's got the mind for it, the love for it. She's so pretty, a ferret can't help but watch what she'll do.

"Mr. Alexopoulos told me it's a hard business, acting," he said. "And a lot of it's indoors. Start early, work late. Over and over, the same scenes. That wouldn't get old for you, Cheye, that wouldn't get . . . ordinary?"

"It's okay to do ordinary, so long as you don't feel *ordinary,"* she quoted. "Monty, I want to be part of something that changes animals' lives. It would be worth the late, and the over-and-over." She looked to her friend, trusted him to know. "I need to try."

He felt his life shifting, turning around the gingham upon the grass. He waited in the silence, finally asked that which matters, to ferrets, more than any other. "It's your highest right?"

Shadows lengthened a fraction till she answered. She touched the dust-blue brim of her hat lower over her eyes. "Yes."

"Big changes coming."

She nodded.

The two friends looked at each other for a long time.

The evening before Cheyenne left for Hollywood was the Harvest Dance, at the Village Hall in Little Paw. Monty and Cheyenne were there, their parents, their friends, Alexopoulos himself, CineMustelid closed for this night, animals from all the countryside round. Ferrets in their best scarves and hats came to dance to the music of fiddle and guitar, lively tunes to make them merry, and fleet of paw.

Arms linked, lithe bodies and graceful tails spun in reels and squares and lines and quarter-dances on a floor carpeted in forest leaves. The friends saw each other flashing by on one star or another. Cheyenne in her blue hat, Monty in his dusted-off brown one, they caught paws and glances for an instant and let go again, they turned with the music and the scents of winter ahead. Of change, ahead.

After a while, Monty disappeared. Cheyenne noticed, whirled herself away from the dance and out the open door from the light of the hall into darkness. She found him sitting on the hitching post by the board sidewalk, leaning against the night.

"Where's my handsome ranchpaw?"

"Hi, Cheye. Just wanted a little quiet."

"It's a wonderful dance."

He nodded.

"Come on," she said, teasing him in the moonlight. "Out with it."

"I like the quiet."

"So what did you learn in your quiet, Monty?"

He thought carefully, his last chance, decided yes. "I learned this."

In his paw, a single mountain daisy, the color of daylight and sky, chosen that afternoon, carried down from their picnic-place in the high country.

"Oh . . ."

"I'm not much on good-byes."

"I know." She watched him under the moon, studying that broad strong face, his mask and whiskers, as though to hold the moment forever.

Time curled and softened about the two like a warm blanket neither wanted to lift. So long had they been friends that they had taken it for granted: we'll never be apart.

At last Monty stood, slipped Boffin's reins from the hitching post. "You have a good trip to California, now . . ."

"Unless I do my best, Monty, I'll never know."

The minutes slowed, but didn't stop for the two ferrets.

He touched the brim of his hat, watching her eyes, a silent good-bye.

She stepped toward him, kissed his cheek. At the very last, her voice a whisper in the dark: "Bye, Monty . . ."

He swung easily up into his saddle, the night closed in, her friend was gone.

In the morning Cheyenne Jasmine Ferret took the train from Little Paw, Montana, destination Hollywood.

One way, no return.

CHAPTER 2

Before the train had chuffed past the Little Paw town limits, before even the rooftop of the Village Hall was out of sight, Cheyenne Ferret knew she was making the biggest mistake of her life.

Her whiskers pressed against the glass of the train window, she looked back at the only familiar land in the world.

So easy to say, "Off to Hollywood!" or even, "Unless I try I'll never know." Now the unknown had changed from a reversible maybe to a certainty ahead.

Her last sight of the peaks above Sable Canyon, did she imagine a silhouette there, a lone delphin and rider, watching her go? She forced herself to look away before the train took the scene from her, blocked it from sight.

The other ferrets in the coach that morning saw her a composed and lovely creature, sitting paws folded, still and straight. They did not see a ferret fighting for her life in deep-water rapids of change.

I don't know where I'll sleep tonight. I don't know where I'll go when I get off the train in Hollywood. I don't know whom I'll meet, what work I'll do to survive, I don't know if I'll ever see a studio lot or a movie set.

I know Montana. I know Mom and Dad and Monty and his folks. I know my bedroom, I know Starlet and Boffin, I know my friends and their delphins. And all of them—*all of them!*—are sliding behind me this moment, rolling away. A tear fell upon her paw. *How can I be such a fool?*

"Ticket, ma'am?" The conductor ferret looked upon her as he would upon his own young sister, but she didn't see, didn't meet his eyes. She looked away, brushed her tears, handed the folded slip: *Little Paw–Denver, Denver–Hollywood.*

She heard the click of his ticket-punch, and when he gave it back there was a hole in the paper, the shape of a heart.

Now she looked up, wondering, and the conductor leaned down, spoke softly to the traveler. "You don't have to know what's waiting. You're guided by your highest right, Cheyenne Jasmine Ferret, and you will be always!"

Eyes wide, she did not respond.

The conductor touched his cap to her and moved toward the next car: "Tickets, please."

How could he know her name? How could he know her future?

Cheyenne melted in mystery. For answer came only muffled steel rhythms beneath her, wheels on track; gentle

swaying of coach; golden Montana rolling swiftly past her window.

She held her ticket, the punched hole casting a heart of sunlight upon her fur.

Hollywood, for Cheyenne Jasmine Ferret, was not what she had expected.

She had walked but a few steps from the Sunset Express when she saw a handsome ferret holding a sign to the debarking passengers: ACTOR?

Puzzled, she stopped and asked.

"It means if you're an actor," he said, "it's your first time in town, we can help. Do you need a place to stay, do you need a portfolio, do you need to know who's shooting what and where's the audition? We can help."

Cheyenne smiled. "I need all the help I can get."

The Young Actors' Home, Cheyenne found, was a well-kept mansion not far from Wilshire Boulevard, a place of many rooms maintained in the old style. It had belonged to silent-film star Beastil Ferret, bequeathed in perpetuity to actors of new generations. Dark-paneled halls swirled with ingenues and character players, comedians and dancers and stunt ferrets. At the first-floor kitchen they took turns cooking meals and being house-parent.

Welcome at once, others remembering their own arrivals, Cheyenne heard it over and again: "You're so *pretty*!" "Glad you're here!" "You're going to do just fine."

All the ferrets confident, each convinced that no other could fill a role meant for himself, they felt no competition. They loaned each other hats and scarves for auditions, even read for the same roles, persuaded that the right animal will always find the part for which she or he was destined.

"Cheyenne?" asked Jerica Ferret, a petite sable, tasting the name. She scanned the room list, found one at the top of the stairs, led the way. "Westerns only, Cheyenne?"

"I hope not westerns only!" The stairs were flowered in carpet the color of forest moss. The walls were flocked scarlet and gold, hint of CineMustelid. "I love the West, but I'm hoping for period pieces, too; drama, comedy, mystery, action."

"Cheyenne's a beautiful name. It may be a little Western for this business, though. See what happens, but if you've got another name you love, or one you've always wanted, now would be a good time to try it on."

Before her portfolio was finished, she sent one of the photos to Monty Ferret, back home. *For my handsome ranchpaw, with me always . . . With love from your Cheyenne.* It would be the last she would sign that name for a very long time.

One day she auditioned for a small role in *The Lady Speaks,* a film about the past century, for the part of the stage manager, a single line: *"We're ready for you now, Placidia."*

Jasmine practiced the words over and again, roommates offering advice and commentary on her delivery.

"We're ready for you now, Placidia." Not authoritative, she decided, not cold, but warm and welcoming, as though she had come to Placidia expecting a gift.

At the audition, the casting director watched her carefully, listened once to the line, no change in her expression, handed Jasmine a card. *Wednesday at six on B.*

The young actress said thank you too late, after the director had moved on to the choice of twin kits from four sets of cute little faces.

She dashed home, throwing open the walnut-and-glass doors of the old mansion.

"I got it! I got the part!"

Others glad, they gathered round, asked her to read the line again just as she had at audition. *Six* meant 6 A.M., they told her, B was the second giant soundstage at Silver Mask Studios.

Wednesday at 5:30 A.M. Jasmine arrived combed and brushed, Stage B, Silver Mask, having presented her card at the gate.

"Good luck, Miss Jasmine," the gateferret had said, and waved her through.

She slipped in the door with the makeup artists.

"You're Jasmine," said one with a smile.

She nodded, a-tremble with butterflies.

"You come with us, sweetheart, and we'll get you all ready for the camera. I'm Mollie, here's Penta and Glorielle."

"This is my first shoot . . ."

"Don't worry," said Glorielle.

Heavy black cables snaked the floor, drops and half-curtains sectioned off the soundstage, video monitors displaying distant sets, empty of action, no one watching. Overhead, a forest of massive floodlights high in the scaffolding, more of them set on great lifts and tripods.

Can I learn this? Will this become my home?

The three sat her down in the makeup room, walls of lights and mirrors, counters for colors and brushes and sponges, they studied her from many angles.

"What do you think, Penta?" asked Mollie. "What a beautiful face! I'd say a light pan, a touch of liner."

"She's got the bones, all right," said Glorielle. "Lovely. And something more . . ."

Penta watched as though Jasmine were a sculpture from a land far over the rainbow.

Finally she shook her head. "A dust of chalk. That's all."

With this, the others looked at the young animal anew, nodding agreement. No pan, no liner for this lovely dark-eyed snow with the indefinable aura. Only a sift of matte, enough to keep the highlights in her coat from strobing on film. Nothing more.

For the first time, Jasmine Ferret felt the pouf of chalk, sniffed its cool fragrance.

One day, thought Penta, watching the mirror, she's going to own this town.

She was pronounced perfect and released. "Don't stand on the red mats, dear, they're setting up the big lights this morning," called Mollie. "Relax! Enjoy!"

The chalk seems to work, thought Jasmine. Heads turned her way on the set, eyes appraising. Whispers.

"Look!"

"Oh, my . . ."

The assistant director was there, the camera operator, the sound crew, crane and dolly operators, electricians moving floods and spots in the catwalks overhead. No one was unaware that somebody new was on the set, and word filtered around that the somebody was named Jasmine.

At last the director arrived, an easy-spoken, toffee-color animal, black mask speckled silver. About his neck Heshsty Ferret had thrown a worn silk scarf, his casual trademark.

He nodded to all, for the set had gone quiet when he appeared. "Good morning, everyone. A few pages, today. Anybody see anything that is *not* going to be fun?"

He looked up, and scanning his colleagues he caught sight of Jasmine, standing alone outside the group. His expression did not change, he said no word. Silent, everyone watching him watching her, he remembered to nod hello to the newcomer.

Politely, she nodded back.

Jasmine had heard the rumor, as had all Hollywood, that Heshsty Ferret was finishing a screenplay so secret that only the title was known. Some claimed that *First Light* would take three films to tell, others thought five. Some knew that Part 1 was titled *Origin,* others had heard *Home Planet.* Beyond that, it was speculation; the tightest-security project in Silver Mask's history centered on this modest director's vision of the far beginnings of his own race.

Jasmine stood twenty paws distant, that morning on the soundstage, listened to Heshsty's outline of the day's shooting.

"As you've seen from the dailies, *The Lady Speaks* is beginning to work rather well. Everybody keep doing today what we did yesterday . . ." He smiled, scanning the shooting script. ". . . keep loving that camera."

He turned to two ferrets standing together in period scarves and hats.

"Millisa and Nolan, you're leading the way for us, this morning. Hold that wonderful tension please, you two, just the way you are. Millisa gets her big scene today, and what we'r . . ."

In the midst of the word, Jasmine heard a snap overhead, a rush and hiss through the air, a blur of a floodlight plummeting to the floor not five paws away, an explosion of blue voltage, blinding, glass and sheet-iron caught in the light's safety shroud.

"*Fang!*" Jasmine ducked, brought her paws up to protect.

Echoes from the shattered light subsided, every eye riveted speechless upon Jasmine Ferret, hearing not the crash but the echo of her sudden oath. No one moved.

"Miss Jasmine," said Heshsty Ferret, his voice level and calm, "this is a soundstage, at a motion picture studio. All of us are happy you're here, we look forward to working with you. Yet we'd appreciate not hearing such language in our workplace, if you don't mind."

She was mortified. Her first day on set, and she had *cursed*! She hoped to say "I'm sorry, sir," but her whiskers quivered, the words stuck in her throat. The best she could do was to shake her head no.

"Thank you," said the director, looking away, back again briefly to Jasmine, then to his leading lady. "Now. Millisa gets her big scene today . . ."

Jasmine didn't shoot her own scene until nearly noon, watched the others, learning fast. She knew her marks and she hit them, stopped a few paws from the leading lady, a look of warm anticipation. "We're ready for you now, Placidia."

Silence. Then five words from Heshsty Ferret: "Cut. Print. Thank you, Jasmine."

No suggestions, no cover-shots, no let's try for one better. She left uncaring even to see the dailies of her scene, convinced that she would never again work in Hollywood.

She could not believe what she had done. *I cursed!* she thought. *On a soundstage!*

She was the only animal in the building who hadn't noticed her eyes, her own luminous vulnerability during her moment on camera, the only one not aware that Heshsty Ferret watched her leave, watched every step she took, all the way off the set.

Such was the intensity of the moment that their names were linked next day in the tabloids. HESHSTY FERRET SAVES INGENUE'S LIFE went the headline in *Possibly So* magazine.

Somewhat more accurately, in the "Hollywood" column of *Maybe:* "There was electricity on the set of Heshsty Ferret's *The Lady Speaks* yesterday as the director made the acquaintance of Jasmine Ferret, newly arrived at Silver Mask from Texas."

CHAPTER 3

Monty Ferret missed Cheyenne more than he would admit. Yet ferrets do not complain, nor do they seek to change the choices of others after a decision's made.

She disappeared West, he stayed at Little Paw. Devoted to delphins, determined to know their language, gradually he came to understand that Boffin's parents had been wild creatures, as fast as the wind. *Monty,* his delphin told him, as best the ferret could sense, *the time's come! I need to race!*

Testing what he heard, Monty turned Boffin loose down a measured prairie straightaway, timed the runs along the thousand- and the ten-thousand-thousand-paw courses. His delphin's race times made Monty blink. To Boffin's delight, they entered nearly every event statewide, the two unbeatable, the talk of delphin-loving ferrets all the way across Montana.

Boffin whickered, turned his head, moved his whiskers just so: *I told you I could run!*

With their winnings, Monty bought Old Gramp Weasel's spread by the Little Paw River, restoring the pine-branch cabin, adding a bunkhouse and tack room. Working alone, he rebuilt the corral, smoothed a racing track on level ground, added a barn.

Came a day just after dawn, as he strained with scaffold and tackle to hoist the key-branch ridge-post aloft:

"Need a paw?"

The visitor had approached so near and quietly before she spoke that Monty startled, nearly let go the rope of his block and tackle. The ridge-beam jerked downward under the scaffold, swayed overhead.

He turned his head as best he could while he hauled, and there to his right stood a small ferret, an animal the color of nutmeg, her mask in shades of clove.

"Thanks," he replied through gritted teeth, creaking the weight of the great branch upward again, a decipaw at a time. "Be with you in a bit." He took a great breath, hauled again.

"Looks heavy," said his visitor.

"Yep." He considered belaying the rope to rest for a while, declined the thought. He would stop hauling when the pole was where it needed to be.

"Can I help?"

Monty smiled, his paws trembling on the rope. Throw her entire weight on the tackle, wouldn't move a straw.

"Yes, you can," he grunted. "Make me stronger!"

"How much stronger?"

At that, Monty began to laugh, the ridge-beam creaking downward as he did. It was all he could do to hold the tension while he forced the rope into a jam-cleat. Its fall arrested, the branch swung ponderously forth and back overhead.

He turned. "Excuse me?"

"How much stronger do you want to be?" The little ferret watched him unsmiling, solemn as a woodchuck.

"Why, strong enough to meet my need."

The stranger nodded approval. "Well said!" She took a step toward him, as though to introduce herself, but instead murmured a quiet comment: "And it's done."

He offered his paw. "Monty Ferret," he said. "What's done?"

"Call me Kinnie. Try your rope."

"In a minute. That's the heavy one, the ridge-beam. The others won't be so bad."

"Try it now."

Why does she insist? Yet he remembered his Courtesies: Respect for elders, respect for peers, respect for kits, respect for self.

Odd, he couldn't tell which she was, his forthright little visitor, for she seemed both wise and young, other and intimate. He honored her nevertheless and did as she asked.

Both paws on the tackle, he took a breath and bore down upon the rope, pulled it free of its cleat. The line was as tight in his paws as had been before, yet barely did he strain to hold the great wooden beam aloft.

Strong enough to meet my need, he had asked, and suddenly it was so. Who is this creature?

Not without effort, but neither with much of it did Monty gather the rope to himself, paw over paw, the monster branch wheeling slowly upward.

Now it swung just above the slots he had cut at the center of the roof-support posts. He eased the rope and one end settled into place, the ridge-beam pivoting about the post till the other end hovered over the notch at the opposite side. Then it dropped home, an echoing thud when Monty slacked the line. Tackle now loose in his paws, the beam required nothing more than a tap of setting-pegs to secure it in place.

"Good barn," said his visitor.

"Thank you. A little stouter than need be."

"No. You'll be glad, this winter."

Monty studied his visitor in silence. How could she know about a winter yet to come? A philosopher ferret, he concluded. Rare animals, mystical and strange, they say. Now here one stands.

"Welcome," he said.

"Thank you for inviting me."

Don't remember inviting, he thought. But I'm curious, of course. Maybe curiosity's the invitation. "I get three wishes?"

"No. One. All else follows."

"I want to know."

"That's your wish?"

He nodded.

"And it's done."

That phrase again, he thought, like a sorcerer's incantation. "What's done?"

"Your wish. It's done. You know."

"I don't feel any different."

"Nothing's changed, but different you are."

"Why?"

She explained, as to a kit, "I give you permission to become aware of what you know."

"Show me."

"Show yourself. I ask, you answer." The little animal moved, now, just a few steps in the dust of the morning, backing away from him as though she planned to become the size of a house. "Who am I, Montgomery Ferret?"

"I'm not sure . . ."

"Wrong. You are sure. You are absolutely certain. But you lack courage to say the unusual." She sighed. "I give you permission to be courageous." Then, patiently: "Who am I, Montgomery Ferret?"

"You're a philosopher ferret."

"Was that so hard? I am, in your terms, a philosopher ferret. *How do you know that?*"

He reached for his truth. "I know." Would she understand?

A smile for the bravery of his answer. From courage, she thought, does wisdom spring.

The nutmeg creature rubbed her paws together, delighted that Monty had allowed her to appear at last. So much to say! "Where do I come from?"

Habit told Monty, *I don't know.* Fear said, *How could I know?* Yet like all ferrets, he tested choices every day against his highest right, and thus had he been led, so far, along his way. His highest right had chosen Montana for his home, had chosen to meet his friend Cheyenne when both were kits. His highest right had let her go toward her destiny as hers had let him go to his. His highest right had lifted a roof beam this morning, and his highest right would find a way to teach his gift to others who cared.

Yet never had he asked for more than guidance, never had he asked his highest self to light those darks unlit by others. Now a lightning bolt: *How can it answer if I don't ask?*

"I'm a philosopher ferret," Kinnie said, quiet patience. "Where do I come from?"

Highest self, he asked silently, where do philosopher ferrets come from?

He didn't have to wait, or to think. "Not from a place." Of course. So simple: "From a direction of spirit," he said, "a direction of caring."

"Yes. Can you come from there?"

"Of course I can," he said. Anyone can.

"Now a quiz. You know that I am a philospher ferret because . . ." She hinted, expecting a certain answer, "Because I leave no . . ."

She wants me to give her words, not mine? Monty tilted his head, puzzled. ". . . stone unturned?"

She frowned. *"Pawprints!* I leave no pawprints!"

Be patient when she veers, he told himself. She wants me to notice.

He looked, and sure enough. In the fine powder-dust, the floor of Monty's barn-to-be, not a mark where she had stepped.

"I leave no pawprints because . . ."

Trusting, accepting her permission to be brave: ". . . because I watch your image within and project it where I will. You leave no pawprints because you are not of my outer world but my inner."

Kinnie inclined her head, almost a bow to him. "Good! Not '*the* outer world,' you said, '*my* outer world'!" She stepped to one side, looked down. "Of course I *could* leave pawprints . . ."

It felt like puzzle pieces falling into place, for Monty, permissions like snowflakes, gentle, unique. He could have explained everything about her that instant, about her and about himself. Of course she could leave pawprints, if she wanted to.

How strange, he thought. Find the greatest teachers, ask the hardest questions, they never say, *Study philosophy,* or, *Get your degree.* They say, *You already know.*

The little ferret watched this in Monty's eyes. "Then where's the school for philosopher ferrets?"

"On the corner," he replied, a smile for the picture he saw, one room in a forest glade, bright curtains at the window, a little chimney. "The school's on the corner of the trail where I ask what I need to know and the road where I realize the answer."

"I like the 'realize' part, Monty. That's the place, all right. And I'm your teacher."

Monty laughed. "No, ma'am. You're the same as me."

"Oh? Indeed." She frowned again, paws akimbo, clove-color fists at her waist. "Don't you mean I am like you, I am similar to you? Not the same as you."

"You're the same as me."

Kinnie was quiet, studying him. When they get the idea, she thought, they get it fast. "And who, then, are your fellow philosopher ferrets?"

Once the answer would have been impossible. "Every creature who cares to ask, finds their own answers."

"Every creature? You mean every *ferret* who cares to ask. Otherwise, philosopher ants? Philosopher humans? Philosopher elephants?"

"No," said Monty. "What's real for elephants is real for ants."

All at once she approached, looked up to him, touched his shoulder. "Not bad, Monty Ferret. It took you a lifetime, but you've got the idea. The fun begins!"

As though she had expected it, a sound behind them. With a jaunty wave the nutmeg ferret vanished. No paw-prints.

Hoofbeats approaching, a delphin whinny, glad to find Monty.

"Whoa down, Lightning," said Jupe Ferret, slowing from a trot around the corner of the ranch house. "He's squared a ridge-beam that'll stand forever, but the kit's gonna need some help to raise her up."

The delphin stopped close enough for Monty to produce a carrot cube from the bag in his tool kit, crunched it happily.

Then Jupe leaned back in his saddle, stared at the great branch set in place above. His whiskers tilted forward. "Well, I declare! Good mornin', Monty."

His cousin touched the brim of his hat. "Jupe."

The rider's eyes did not waver from the beam at the roof peak. "Before dawn, you moved that piece up there? On your own?"

"Nope," said Monty. "Had some help."

From his flood of learning had bobbed a caution: sometimes we'd best keep quiet about what we know. Fast as light within, he thought, but outside, let's take her one step at a time.

☁

So it was, that summer, that Monty Ferret opened his own Western riding and racing school, mostly for kits but grown-ups welcome.

Alonetimes, he practiced asking questions of his higher self, came to realize, day by day, what he had long believed was true—ferrets have powers they haven't begun to touch. Other times he taught riding, and the language of delphins.

"First thing," he told each new class, gathered round the starting line, "you're going to learn how to lose a delphin race."

And they did. They practiced all ways to be graceful in defeat, invented new ones, how to honor those delphins and ferrets who rode faster than they, to cherish challenge and strategies well planned. Monty Ferret taught them to ask winners for advice with such open sincerity that advice was freely given.

Last and least, he taught them to race and win.

Hidden within were the greater lessons: animals are equals; how to meet with them in places of the mind; to link spirits toward ends mutually wished.

Others came to listen, asked for more. Finally Monty took time to record what he had learned and how he had learned it, his calm, earnest voice telling stories to a microphone.

With *Secrets of the Delphins,* the tapes released, it turned out that it didn't matter whether his listeners rode delphins or not. It was Monty's adventure that mattered, his humor, his homespun common sense. His stories entertained ferrets who would never touch a delphin or even see one.

Softly, then, began a snow of listener mail to Little Paw from around the world, and in it, one day, a heavy envelope postmarked Loch Y'ar, Scotland.

⌢

Dear Brother, wrote Zander Ferret. *What grand discoveries, Monty, congratulations! Secrets of the Delphins is unique, original, fascinating to hear. You're changing the way we think about delphins, the way we treat animals everywhere.*

Zander told of his own adventures, too, a zoologist abroad.

It is the most wonderful news. We have managed to clone a new type of miniature sheepling, less than a quarter the size of your smallest delphin. Of warm and dear disposition, their minds link as one when they wish. They are intelligent, thoughtful, reflective. Their wool is long-strand, in colors to rival the purest of nature every shade of the rainbow, pastels to brights, and absolutely fast.

We've applied your principles, Monty, about listening to our little sheep. At first we were amazed, but although they are romantics, we've found that they are shrewd business animals as well.

In short, the Rainbows have agreed to contract for their wool, on condition that they find suitable accommodations at a resort in the high country of the Wild West, as they describe it, Wyoming or Montana. They prefer open lands with weathers and views conducive to abstract thought and light exercise, in the care of ferret guides. Their outdoor skills are poor.

They would require accommodations for two thousand sheep, along with a few pipers and drummers of whom they've become quite fond, Scottish ferrets skilled at Highland airs.

Your work has convinced us that my own brother is the one ferret to establish and operate a top-quality ranch, catering to the needs and wishes of this unique culture. Of course the ranch would include expanded facilities for your racing schools and delphin studies, at whatever level you wish.

After several pages of a careful business and financial analysis, his brother concluded:

In short, dear Monty, you'll be fascinated with the character and qualities of the Rainbows. I wonder if you might respond as soon as you receive this letter, that you will travel to meet the sheep and discuss their offer and ours in person.

Ever your affectionate,

Zander

Montgomery Ferret put the letter down on his barn-wood desktop, ran his paws slowly over his muzzle and ears, creaked back in his chair, closed his eyes.

Highest right, he asked, what to choose? I'm no sophisticated businessferret, I'm a ranchpaw, I love Montana. If I say yes to Zander, will I enrich lives or disappoint them? If I say no, will I be dashing hopes or shifting them toward a better path? How is it that I can meet their needs and mine, too?

His highest right responded at once, four words:

Will it be fun?

The storm of his choice overwhelmed Montgomery Ferret almost but not quite.

It rose up from a thousand megapaws of prairie and forest and river and mountainside, in the wilderness to the north and east of Little Paw, by the village of Northstar. The entrance was marked with a heavy arch of curved timber across the road, letters carved into black pine, filled with white clay:

MONTY FERRET'S RAINBOW SHEEP RESORT
and
RANCHPAW TRAINING CENTER

The land swarmed with construction ferrets, rang with the sound of hammers and saws, the grate of stone on stone as chimneys rose from ground to sky, the creak and thud of fine straight branches becoming walls, the clank of chinking irons, the scrape of wooden furniture on wide-plank floors.

Then it was finished, no longer a model landscape in the trailer office but full-size to the horizon. Here the staff quarters and ranchkit training grounds, bunkhouses and barns, corrals and racing tracks and dining hall. A distance away nestled cluster on cluster of rustic branch cabins for the Rainbows, meditation centers, hot tubs and picnic spots, towers for pipes and drums to call the sunset.

The higher delight for the little sheep, however, the dream that had called them here, was the wilderness of untamed Montana.

He had hoped to share his joy of the land with one other, but destiny had taken her from his sight. Now he would share that country with thousands.

CHAPTER 4

Blue flames erupted near table seven, swirled at the edge of a party of twelve. Masks and whiskers at other tables turned to watch, celebrities from the highest tiers of the land murmured to each other, every entrée a performance.

Gerhardt-Grenoble Ferret lofted his grand Midnight Omelet in the fire, called down a meteor shower, dust of saffron and coriander through the flames, deftly slipped his creation, still afire, to all. Fragrance irresistible.

"Voilà," he said. *"Bon appétit, mesdames et messieurs."* A sad smile, a bow and wave to the cultured applause, a nod, as he left, to personal friends among the dazzling guests. No one noticed, as he walked away, that the chef seemed lost in thought, as if behind the smile he were saying good-bye.

It could not be said that Manhattan's La Mer des Étoiles was Gerhardt-Grenoble's flagship restaurant. They were all flagships, those haute-dining spots in Paris, in Beverly Hills, in Tokyo and Buenos Aires and Nuku Hiva. When ferrets play at high society, they do so with perspective and delight, and they found in the wonder-chef a superstar the equal of his patrons.

"Magic," whispered the waiter at table seven. "Here is no cook, here is the magician, no?"

Early mornings, before dawn, no matter where he was in the world, it was the habit of Gerhardt-Grenoble to don scarf and cap, visit the finest markets of the city; to sniff and touch the freshest fruits and vegetables, through all the raucous bustle of the morning. He did so this day in Manhattan with his oldest friend and partner, the two nodding to proprietors for this carton or that tray, newly picked, to be shipped to La Mer. They moved from stand to stand through the stalls, noses twitching in currents of fragrance. The world is a kitchen, he thought, a chef's at home anywhere on the planet.

"Hup, hup, hya," called the banana ferrets, tossing the heavy fruits one to another from cargo container to display. *"Hup, hup, hya!"*

"La belle cuisine," said the chef, gentle Swiss accent over the noise. "It has brought us a long way together, Armond."

"A long way, indeed, from your first kitchen," replied his partner. "It will bring us a long way yet." Armond sniffed a tomato the color of deep-sky sunset, put it down, chose from another tray, sniffed again, nodded to the watchful merchant ferret.

The merchant saw the nod, noted the carton number on his order form.

"You'll do well," said the chef.

Armond turned to his friend, lifted his chin a fraction, listening. "Gren?"

From a scarf pocket Gerhardt-Grenoble drew forth a newspaper story, folded in half, offered it without comment.

His partner opened the clipping and read. *THE WOOLLY WEST: MONTGOMERY FERRET'S RAINBOW SHEEP RESORT ONLY SOURCE OF FABULOUS FLEECE.*

A few lines down, a photo of Monty holding a Rainbow lamb, then the story from the newspaper torn through, as though the reader hadn't cared what followed the headline.

Armond looked from the clipping to Gerhardt-Grenoble, expressionless. "You're leaving."

"Yes. Our agreement."

"I haven't forgotten. Either one of us. For any reason."

"La Mer is yours. Worldwide."

"Gren, you are at the top of your powers! This is what you want?"

The chef nodded. The proprietor, watching, saw the nod, made note to deliver two dozen red zucchini to La Mer.

"It will happen to you, Armond. There comes a time when we are called to surpass technique. And technique can only be surpassed by . . . what?"

"Warmth? Style? That certain *la*?"

"No. *Simplicity!*"

"Simplicity. Of course. But for simplicity you do not have to leave all that you have created. You go where? To . . ." Armond glanced at the clipping . . . "Montgomery?"

A smile. "To Montana."

"Your fame will follow you. Your reputation."

"No. Gerhardt-Grenoble was last seen . . . come to think of it, Armond, you yourself were the last animal to see him. Promise that you shall never tell where he went."

"How long? Will you return?"

"Enjoy La Mer."

There's an old ferret proverb: *Having climbed certain peaks we descend no more, but spread our wings and fly beyond.*

The two animals were quiet amid the *hup-hup-hya*'s, the callings and tumults of the market. Then the chef turned, nodded good-bye to his friend and disappeared into the crowd.

When one is a genius, thought Armond, one is often a little crazy.

CHAPTER 5

"Hup . . . hup . . . hya!"

At the command, a line of ranchkits hurled their soft Rainbow-wool lassos at a row of wooden sheep, fluffed out with hay. Every noose amiss, bounced off targets or fallen short in the dust.

The ranchpaw instructor shrugged good-naturedly, the ferret kits pulling in their colorful lariats, turning to listen.

Gerhardt-Grenoble Ferret noticed this, stepped from the ranch taxi into Montana summer, sniffed the sage and pine and wildflowers.

"When you hear *hya,*" said the instructor, lean and prairie-wise, "the lasso wants to fly *over* the sheep. It wants to go over your sheep's neck instead of onto a nearby rock or bush. Someday, that saw-sheep could be a Rainbow wandered to the edge of a ravine or a gorge, your lasso's going to save its

life. So we need to practice, don't we?" He showed them, backing away and away, an impossible distance, the kits thought, from his target.

"Not too far, Dakota!" one ranchkit cried, the others hushing her at once.

"Now make sure to carry the fall of the lariat a good way round from the slip to your paw," he called, whirling his azure lasso overhead, "so it'll snake on out after you let 'er go. Like . . . so . . . !"

The chef found the ranch office, a door marked *Monty Ferret,* and knocked.

"It's open."

He entered. The rancher looked younger than his photo in the newspaper. Broad of face and smoothly muscled, he was leaning over a ledger on his desk, at which sat a businessferret, her back to the door.

Gerhardt-Grenoble blinked. On the desk was a photo of Jasmine Ferret, an inscription he couldn't quite read.

Monty looked up from the ledger. "Howdy."

What was a photo of his celebrity friend doing in the wilderness of Montana? The chef blinked again, recovered his composure. "Howty." The word came out more Swiss than Western.

"How can we help you, today?"

"I'm your new chef."

The rancher smiled. "That's very nice, Mister . . ."

"Call me Cookie."

"That's very nice, Cookie, and I thank you for the thought, but we've already got a chef."

"Good. He'll want to be my assistant."

Monty laughed, ran a paw back from his forehead, smoothing the fur. "Bud's going to want to be your assistant?"

Cookie nodded.

"And maybe you want to tell me why Bud's going to want to be your assistant when he's already head cook, has been since we built the ranch?"

"I'll show you why."

Monty Ferret stroked his whiskers with a paw. "You'll show me."

"Yes."

Monty smiled again. "How are you going to show me?"

Cookie raised his eyebrows. "I will need three eggs."

Now the businessferret turned, amused at his words. Her dark mask delicately chiseled, eyes like cool ebony, missing nothing.

"This is Adrienne," said Monty, "our business manager." He laid a pencil for a bookmark in the ledger. "As a matter of fact, I believe we may have some eggs. Maybe Bud will lend a few."

Adrienne, still smiling, offered her paw.

CHAPTER 6

Montgomery Ferret rode Ladyhawke slowly and quietly in the dawn toward the high range, black woolen lariat coiled by his saddle horn, bedroll behind. Silent paints splashed the sky eastward, the air cold and sharp. He breathed deep.

It was breathing light itself, light and the cool saps of pine and sage and fir, of earth and grass mixed with the scents of pure river, of wildflower touched by the gentlest breeze.

Love it, he thought. Never get tired of this, never will.

He breathed again. He smelled distance in the air, the fragrance now of meadow grass as he rode to the Halfway Meadows, then the hint of Strawberry, now Citron and Peach, Tangerine and Blueberry and Licorice and Apricot.

Apricot ran to meet him, a sheep just a few paws high, bright color of fresh fruit and tantalizing fragrance to match.

Let's see what he wants, Ladyhawke, thought Monty. His delphin stopped, no word or touch. The rancher dismounted, reached a paw to the little clone. "Hi, Apricot! You're havin' a good time, are you?"

The Rainbow edged forward, a small Scottish reply in the rancher's mind: Monty, *we're lost*!

The ferret rubbed the sheep behind its ears. "How about that. You're lost again, are you?"

Apricot nodded. Aye.

"Ranchpaws been giving the classes, have they, on your outdoor savvy? *Orientation and Landmarks? Reading the Trail?*"

Aye.

"And we haven't been paying too much attention, have we?"

There were bonny wee blooms by the tarn, Monty, we could n'a pay attention!

Came the sound of tiny hooves, the fragrance of Lime and Plum and Cherry, then the animals themselves, pure colors to match.

Following them their guide, a ranchkit upon a delphin considerably smaller than Ladyhawke, bandanna tied about his neck, an earth-color wide-brim hat.

"Good morning, sir," said the kit.

"'Morning, Budgeron. How're your Rainbows doing?"

"Fine, sir. Everyone was up to watch the sunrise, today. After a bit we'll be moving down to the lower meadows, then back to the ranch."

Monty eased up into his saddle. "Everybody's happy?"

"Yes, sir, they seem to be. We'll have a little skip rope this morning, sir. And they'd like to splash in the river a bit."

"You'll be careful for the cold."

"Yes, sir. We've got towels and robes for them in the wagon, they can ride back to the ranch, if they want. But with their wool getting as long as it is, and being Rainbows, they'll stay warm. I don't suspect we'll have many riders, sir."

"I'd reckon not." Monty smiled for the youngster's grown-up talk, for his earnest responsibility. Budgeron Ferret was a city kit, but had taken to the land and its challenges. He had an ear for language and a way with words, an easy grace with them that required only vision and practice to perfect.

"You're taking notes, are you, Budgeron?"

"Notes, sir?"

"Montana. The sky, the rivers. What everyone says when they're talking. What you think about it. You're taking it all down."

The kit tilted his hat back, looked up at the rancher. "Why, yes, sir, I am."

"Do you know who you are, Budgeron?"

The kit looked away, thoughtful, back again. "I've got my hopes, sir . . ."

"You don't mind work, if it's hard enough?"

The kit shook his head. Was Monty Ferret reading his future?

"Then chances are, those hopes will be coming true. Not words, are going to lead you, as much as *ideas,* wouldn't you think?"

"I don't know, sir."

"You know, Budgeron. You may not be aware, but *you know.*"

Monty gave no command that the ranchkit could discern, but Ladyhawke began to walk away, and her rider didn't look back.

Left alone, the sheep turned to the kit as though to ask where are we, Budgeron? Where are we going now?

The young rider shook his head, touched the coil of his crimson lariat, a gift of wool from Strawberry. I know my own future? Why not? If Monty Ferret says so, why not?

"This way, please," he said to the Rainbows. They were enjoying the scenery. "Tangerine? Apricot? Come on, everybody. This way."

"Noodles 'n Sauce! Hear, you ranchkits, ranchpaws . . . Noodles 'n Sauce!"

Cookie's ferret-metal triangle clanged from his chuckwagon through the last of the afternoon as the kits finished rounding the Rainbows, gentling them into their camp for a night unseasonably cold, setting oat treats in bowls by their bedrolls.

Nearby, big Jupe Ferret finished writing for the day, closed his notebook, tucked it into his saddlebag by a paperback classic worn nearly through: Avedoi Merek's *The Ferret Way*. He rode the short distance to the chuckwagon, dismounted near the waterhole, let loose his delphin, Lightning, to drink.

"Noodles 'n Sauce is it again?" He enjoyed Cookie's humor. No matter the entrée, no matter the exquisite fragrance or exotic taste conjured from the simplest ingredients, the chef's blackboard menu read the same.

"Every day's not too often for Noodles 'n Sauce." Then the chef looked at him, testing, refining his Western accent with Swiss precision. "Should I be saying *ever* day, Jupe? Must I drop the terminal *y*?"

"*Every* day's just fine, you're doin' fine, Cookie." A rare smile, and a question never answered twice the same: "Where *do* you come from, by the way?"

Now the first of the ranchpaws arrived, and the chef served their meals smoothly, expertly, on tin plates. He grinned at the big ferret. "East Montana."

Jupe shook his head, muttered, "Yep. About Zurich east, I'd wager." Cook's got a right to his secrets, he thought.

This evening, Noodles 'n Sauce was forest-mushroom soufflé à la Niçoise, light as fair-weather cloud, surrounded by fresh-roasted vegetables upon a bed of wild rice. A barrel of mountain-water stood on the chuckwagon, and dippers to refill the brimming cups.

Soon dozens of kits and 'paws converged from the cold about the chuckwagon, their delphins free to graze, stories of the day flying above the blue gingham cloth Cookie had spread near the campfire. Plates in paw, cups on the ground, the clink of forks and wonder at the tastes. A chorus of "Mmm" and "Delicious!" and "Well done, Cookie!" rang out, as ever it did, come mealtimes.

Sunset a final glow in the air, ranchkits circled the fire to hear the old-timers tell what they had seen in the wild, some of the stories true.

One ranchpaw, Dakota Ferret, stayed out upon his delphin, Shadow, awake in the near-freezing dark, standing guard in case a night-walking Rainbow should wander near the cliffs. He'd take his supper later.

From the busy day and crisp prairie air, the Rainbows were clustered and asleep save Violet, whose habit it was to contemplate long into the night.

Cookie stood quietly by his wagon sideboard, testing the soufflé, testing his assistant, Bud: would the tiniest pinch of saffron have improved the work?

Bud was a changed ferret from not so long ago. Cooking, once his job, had become his passion.

"I'd choose no for the saffron. However, do you think a trace of *cumin,* Chef?"

Cookie smiled. There is promise, here.

Jupe fetched his verse book from his saddlebag, plied on with pencil in the firelight, half-listening to the stories, writing slowly, verse after verse of epic rhyme. The day that Monty married, if ever that day would come, this rare-spoken 'paw planned to recite for the bride a first-hand history of his cousin.

Old Barclay Ferret finished his tale "The Last Lion in Great Falls County," calculated that the kits were properly amazed. He could see their breath in the chill, as they looked this way and that for great cats in the dark. The story was a little scary, he had to admit.

"Well, what're we here for, kits?" he asked, by way of restoring their mettle. "We're here for . . ."

"Action!" called the youngsters together.

"We're here for . . ."

"Adventure!"

"We're here for . . ."

"Romance on the high plains!"

"And as you seek," said the ranchpaw, finishing the ritual, "so shall you find."

He tilted his head toward Jupe. "Go on . . . ask," he said, and at last the ranchkit Alla called across the campfire, a little voice, "Will you read to us, Jupe? Will you read what you've written so far?"

The ferret looked up from his bent pages. "The whole of it?"

"If you would."

"Nope. I'd rather not."

The other ranchkits asked, Percifal and Boa, Budgeron and Kayla and Strobe, one after the other. "Will you read to us, Jupe?"

Patiently, his reply to each: "Thank you, no." "Poem's not for kits."

Then Cookie, from the chuckwagon, while Bud ground seeds of cumin: "Monty's with the flocks on the south range tonight, Jupe. You can read your story. They won't make a word of it to him. Will you, kits?"

The bulky ranchpaw looked up from his verse book to the young ferrets, narrowed his eyes. "You'll tell no one? Not a word? I'll not have anyone giving away that Jupe's doing a poem to surprise him, someday. That's a promise?"

The kits looked at each other; Strobe spoke for them all: "Promise."

"Well, then . . ." Jupe shifted his bandanna, turned it so that the faded flower-pattern rag hung at the back of his neck instead of the front, the better for reading. He turned the battered pages to the beginning, glinted at the kits suspiciously. "You're sure you want to hear this . . ."

The kits nodded solemnly. Ranchpaws shared secret smiles. Nothing Jupe liked better than to read his rhymes to the young ones.

Cookie brought the kitchen lantern nearby, brighter than the light of embers, and Jupe Ferret began to read the history of his cousin Montgomery. If asked, he'd allow it might have been maybe a little romanticized, but mostly the poem was the way he had watched it happen.

He took a sip of mountain-water, looked one more time to the kits. They nodded. Go ahead, Jupe.

He began in a deep slow voice under the stars, a voice like woodsmoke, as seasoned by weathers as was the animal himself. Off in the distance a nighthawk whirred in the sky.

"Now Monty was born with the wind in his fur," he read,
And a taste of the wild in his eyes.
If you knew him back then, you'd have thought right away
Here's a kit who's uncommonly wise."

He looked up, saw masks and whiskers pointed to him, rapt attention.

"His dad was a rancher, his mom was a muse,
Expect an unusual kin.
A wonder with delphins, at home on the plains
And knowing The Way from within.

"He grew up a-ridin', a-ropin' an' such
He grew up a-teachin' it, too.
And one of his students her name was Cheyenne,
The most beautiful ferret he knew."

The kits stirred. Monty had been in *love*?

Jupe cleared his throat.

"The two they were friends from the start, don't you see,
Two kits of the forest and streams.

The boy with the wisdom of nature inside,
The girl with her Hollywood dreams.

"They thought right at first that together they'd stay,
Two pals, all that fun—they would share it!
But it happened in time, for some reason and rhyme,
They'd part for a while, and they'd bear it.

"So Monty went off to his delphins and range,
Cheyenne to her cameras and stages,
He gave of his heart to perfect what he knew,
She gave of her soul to the ages.

"As Miss Jasmine Ferret she won all our hopes,
In her eyes we saw our own yearnings.
We saw her, we loved her—as simple as that,
On the screen we shared her bright learnings."

The ranchkits stared at each other. *Jasmine Ferret!*

"Now many a kit took wings from her scenes,
Many a high dream was founded
On Jasmine's pure vision of what we become
When we know that our spirit's unbounded.

"The price that she paid to deliver her gift
The price that she paid for her glory
Was loneliness, wishing that Monty were there
To be a dear part of her story."

Oh, my, thought the kits. *Monty and Jasmine Ferret!*

"And as for that ferret adrift on plains?
As for Monty himself t'was decreed
He'd give to young ferrets all that he knew
Of endurance and power and speed.

"Of how to bear up when the going gets hard,
Of how to hang on when it's tough,
To care for the ones who're depending on you
To know when enough is enough.

"Then one day it happened, a letter from far,
Request that he'd take a strange mission.
The Rainbows from Scotland's chilly Loch Y'ar
All had the same odd ambition:

"To live in Montana, they said, to a one,
To see the Wild West and its wonder
To camp out in starlight and moonlight and plain,
To camp out in lightning and thunder.

"'Twas adventure they sought, those flocks from the Loch,
The wilderness to them was calling,
They offered to trade their fine wool—give it free
In return for a life so enthralling.

"So a bargain was struck, 'tween Monty and they,
Since they so wished for the sport,
He'd show them the life they dreamed of and more,
He'd open a Rainbow Resort!

"And open it did, the following June,
Surrounded by high-plain serenity,
With ranchkits to guide them, and ranchpaws to trust,
And every sheep-wished amenity.

"Now Rainbows are different, they tend to drift off,
Follow philosophy's quest,
But dangers there are on the plains, in the hills,
They need to be careful, lest:

"Off the cliffs they tumble and fall,
Off in the rivers they sweep,
Off in the desert they wander at all
Off into caverns, no peep

"To be heard, again from those Scots
Who chose high adventure that day,
Who trusted their Monty and threw in their lots
Thinking it all to be play.

"So safety's the foremost concern of their host,
Safety and sheep-lovin' fun.
Those ranchkits and ranchpaws they prize that bright
    wool,
But know commerce is only but one

"Of the elements, part of the deal
They entered with Monty that day,
The others were learning, adventure, and growth,
For sheep now embarked on The Way."

From the icy dark, a low thunder.

"Sheep-whisperer, they called him, because of the sense Monty had, his knowledge of animals' thought . . ."

Jupe looked up; the thunder came louder now, approaching. Cookie and Bud looked northward, the chuckwagon's pots and pans trembling, tins against coppers and steels. Earthquake?

All were on their paws, now, their delphins whiffering, moving toward the safety of the campfire.

Jupe dropped the verse book: *"Stampede!"*

The ground was thundering steadily now, louder.

"Rainbows?" said Cookie. *"Stampede?"*

There was no place to run. The great flock poured out of the night, a tidal wave of woolly bodies, pounding across the plains, a cloud of dust behind them in the dark, up the rise toward the ranchpaws.

Tending the gentle animals, no ferret had thought of Rainbow sheep as a force of nature, yet now they raced south, unstoppable in a tempest of hooves.

The ferrets stood and watched dumbfounded in frosty moonlight. Rainbows gone mad? But we *love them*! They won't trample us down! To the youngest kit, they believed, and trusted. Each stood quietly, watched the cascade of animals approaching high speed in the dark.

At the instant the stampede would engulf the camp and their guides, not ten paws from the chuckwagon, the stampede stopped, Violet in the lead, breathing hard.

Behind her were Apricot and Blueberry, Citron, Peach, Orange and Huckleberry, the scents of flower and spice and fruit around them in a sea of fragrance all at odds with the urgency of the animals. The Rainbows halted, the cloud of dust did not, rolling past to fog them all and dim the moon.

Big Jupe strode forward. "What's on? What's the matter, Rainbows?"

No answer. Danger, Jupe sensed, or tragedy. If Monty were here, he'd have known the matter in an instant. As it was, the sheep stood a panting multicolor mass, fixing the ferrets with their gaze. Then all at once they turned right about, broke into a run, reverse-stampeding north down the slopes, the way they had come.

Jupe whistled for Lightning. "C'mon, 'paws!" he cried to the others as he mounted. "They need us to follow them back!"

A flurry of whistles and cries, ranchpaws and kits mounting up, all the ferrets flying northward, a stampede of their own after the ground-shaking herd.

Wild riding it was under the moon, delphins topspeed over broken ground, leaping rocks and fissures they wouldn't dare in daylight, spray flying as they galloped through the Oat Creek shallows. Yet so tuned to the moment were the ferrets that even ranchkits rode sure and straight through the dark. Something was terribly wrong, and their job was to make it right, not to stumble and be lost themselves.

Jupe rode hard through the midst of that tossing sea of sheep, fleet Lightning passing them left and right. *They're going for the cliffs!*

The herd thundered past its sleeping-meadow straight toward the rock falls beyond. *Where's the cliff-watch? Where's Dakota?*

The rider was nowhere in sight, and without him . . .

"Hyo! Rainbows!" Jupe bellowed. *"Cliffs! Cliffs! You Rainbows hold up now! Hyo! Whoa down!"* There was no response, not a sheep slowed.

Got to get ahead of the stampede, he thought. *Go, Lightning!* Get ahead, get the leaders stopped . . .

Jupe did not consider that if he succeeded, if he outraced the stampede but could not stop the Rainbows, he and his delphin would go first over the cliffs.

Now he was nearly to the front rank of the stampede; there was Violet, bounding, racing.

Too late. The cliffs yawned black ahead. He needed seconds more.

In that instant Violet, in that instant the entire herd of Rainbows stopped, all at once, before the cliff. Abruptly Lightning broke through the first line of sheep, all she could do to keep herself from falling. But stop she did, rocks and pebbles from her four-hoof slide tumbling on over the edge.

Jupe swung down. *"Violet!* What's goin' on, honey?"

The Rainbow looked at him, panting heavily, took a step forward, her nose pointing into the dark, looked back to Jupe. Swiftly arrived the other ferrets, off their delphins to the ground.

Violet took another step toward the cliff, fixed the ranchpaw with her eyes, blinked again beyond.

Jupe followed her gaze. The earth at the cliff was razorsharp, fresh and new. The noose of a blue woolen lasso lay on the ground, its line trailing over the edge.

"Dakota!"

Jupe spun into action, called the nearest ferrets. "Barclay! Strobe! Boa! The cliff's caved, Dakota and Shadow's gone over the edge! We're going to need some lines to hold, goin' down. Alla, Budgeron, you come with me. Let's go!"

At once Jupe disappeared over the sharp break of the rock, his lariat hitched to Barclay's delphin, the ranchkit Alla following. Down the steep rubble they slid in the moonlight, rocks bounding and falling around them, each of the ferrets with a lariat cinched about their shoulders, lines straining upward.

At the end of the slide they found Shadow, nearly covered in rock and sand. A few paws beyond, protected by the body of his delphin, lay Dakota Ferret, thrown clear, unmoving. Alla ran to the ranchpaw, touched his head, put her ear to his chest.

"He's alive, Jupe. His head's cut, he's awfully cold, but he's got a heartbeat."

"Take your bandanna . . ." said Jupe, but Alla had already done so, whipped the cloth from about her neck, doubled it twice, placed it gently over the wound, tied it tight.

"How's Shadow?" she asked.

Jupe and Budgeron heaved themselves against the rubble over the fallen delphin, sweeping it away layers at a time. Shadow blinked awake as the weight came off, gasped for air, lifted its head toward Dakota.

"He'll be fine," said Jupe to the delphin. "So'll be you. Just lay still, let us get this stuff off you, here . . ."

The delphin breathed quick, shallow breaths, obeyed the ranchpaw, lay quiet.

Dakota Ferret moved his head. "Alla . . . Jupe. The cliff . . ."

"Shhh," said Alla. "Not now. Be still."

"I'm all right."

"Yes. Just be still."

As the rocks lifted from the delphin it twisted, found its feet, rose abruptly, shaking its mane in a cloud of pebbles and sand.

"Wind knocked out of you, Shadow . . ."

A step or two toward its rider, the animal wobbled but did not fall. It breathed deep, exhaled dust.

"May I at least sit up, ma'am?" Dakota reached to his head, touched the bandage.

"No," said Alla. "In a minute. Not now. Don't move."

The ranchpaw smiled at that, this kit ordering him about. But he lay where he was, near frozen but glad to be alive.

At the top of the cliff, young Boa had fashioned a knotted-loop bosun's chair from a doubled lariat, passed its lines to the rescue team over the saddle of his delphin braced at the clifftop. Without proper sheerlegs and tackle, he knew, his harness couldn't hoist the injured creatures clear, but the rig provided a near-weightless lift for what would have been a hard climb up the wall of rock.

By dawn the two animals had been made as comfortable as possible, shivering under blankets, warming near the campfire. Cookie fixed a steaming broth of whole-grain-and-vegetable ratatouille for Dakota, Bud made a bowl of hot dandelion oats and sprouted wheat-grass for Shadow. Circling the camp ranged the Rainbows, their own sunrise in the early light, concerned for the welfare of the watch ferret and his delphin.

No sooner had the two ceased to shiver than came a sound of hooves from the trail south, and before long a quiet word. "H'lo, all. How're we doing?"

Monty Ferret dismounted, raised a paw to Dakota and to Shadow, stay still. He looked to the ranchpaw's wound, blood soaking through the proper bandage Alla had placed there.

Instead of inspecting the damage, however, Monty closed his eyes for half a minute, knelt there unmoving. There's nothing here but perfect, he thought. Perfect expression of perfect life: can't be changed, no different truth. Then he turned to the delphin and knew the same, though it seemed to the others as if he preferred to examine the trouble with eyes closed than open.

Jupe shot a glance to Cookie, to see if he noticed the strange action.

The chef caught his eye, raised his brow, nodded slowly. Interesting, he thought. Montgomery Ferret is more than he appears.

Monty rose. "Reckon you two may pull through all right," he said. "How'd you come to think that hoppin' off cliffs would be a good idea?" He had no way of knowing, but he knew.

Dakota had opened his mouth to explain, but Violet pushed forward to stand by Monty. He nodded to her, reached down to stroke her twilight wool.

"I suspect this one had something to do with it? She was walking in the dark, maybe, thinking about the universe, not watching too well where she was going?"

"I'm sorry, Monty," said Dakota. "She got past before I saw her. She was nigh the edge when I got m' lasso on her, pulled her away. Thought the incident was all over, started to go to her when the ground plumb went out from under us, Shadow and me, in a sudden th' air was full o' rocks. Next I knew I woke up powerful cold and pained and here was little Alla, tyin' up m' head and"—he smiled at the kit—"and givin' me orders."

The Rainbow stepped to the injured ranchpaw, brought her face close to his.

"Violet's awful sorry, Dakota," said Monty. "She wishes for all the world she'd have gone off some other direction."

"Sorry for nothin', Violet." The ranchpaw rubbed the sheep behind her ears. "We're both of us just doin' our job, and we best both be careful, 'round those edges!"

The fluffy animal looked to Monty.

"Violet appreciates your greatness of heart. She thanks you kindly for saving her life."

"'S nothin'," said the ranchpaw. "If she hadn't run for the camp, run back and brought the 'paws along, we'd be lying out there still, me and Shadow, gone to ice by now." He breathed her fragrance. "We saved each other's lives, Violet. That's always a pleasure."

Later, the Rainbows crowded together in the sunlight to see the collapsed earth, staying behind ropes the ferrets had laid on the ground a safe distance from the edge. They remarked to each other in their silent language about the excitement in the night, peril and adventure in the dark, just as they had known the Wild West would be. What a life!

Thought flashed in kaleidoscopic patterns through the little clones, relief that Violet and Dakota and his delphin had survived, that the adventure had all worked out for the best. The horror of the earth opening up, their run for help, the thunder of their hooves over sand and rock.

They had never run so before, and the sound of it, *the sound of it!*

Away from the camp, standing upon a rock outcrop, Apricot relived that desperate wonderful stampede, the wind of it beginning in her mind, moving her hooves in slow-time to match. The rhythm echoed to the others: *clak-clak!* clik, clik, clik . . . *clak-clak!* clik, clik, clik . . .

The other clones felt it too, knowing her thoughts. They moved to bare rock places, augmenting with their own hooves Apricot's earthy dance. They joined in, following her lead on the first two beats only, the little sheep herself following with a solo triple-beat:

Clak-clak! stamped the first few Rainbows.

clik, clik, clik . . . Apricot tapped on the rock.

CLAK-CLAK!! Other sheep ran to join, more on more.

clik, clik, clik . . .

CLAK-CLAK!!!

The sheep were absorbed, watching the sound in their linked minds as well as hearing it over the rocks, through the earth itself. Then, as Rainbows do, they began to innovate:

clik-ity-clik-ity-clik . . . tapped Apricot.

CLAK-ITY-CLAK-ITY, CLAK, CLAK-CLAK!!! stamped the flock.

clikity-clikity clik, clik-clik!

CLAKITY-CLAKITY CLAKITY-CLAKITY CLAKITY-CLAKITY CLAKITY CLAKITY-CLAK!!!!

clikity-clikity, clikity-clikity, clikity-clikity, clikity-clik!

Then Apricot and flock began weaving their parts together, solo and chorus intermingled: *CLAKITY* clikity *CLAKITY!* clikity *CLAKITY!!* clikity *CLAKITY-CLAK-ITY, CLAKITY-CLAKITY,* clikity-clikity-clik: *CLAK-CLAK!!!*

With the last beat the Rainbows stood still as noon, listened to the sound of their hooves echoing up the canyons. It sounded like applause, from the hills. When the sheep looked up, they saw it was: a ring of ranchpaws and ranchkits clapping and whistling, tingling with the rhythm, yearning to be Rainbows themselves, and join the dance.

The little animals looked at each other, silent pleasure. What fun! If we sort ourselves now by colors, they thought, then wheel the colors in squares and lines and angles . . .

Thus from tragedy averted was born the Montana Rainbow Zouave Rhythm March Corps and Scottish Dance Company.

The cliffs haunted Monty. Not for their danger, for all would be more careful in rugged country than ever before. The cliffs haunted into a mirror of a different time, slipped loose from where he had tucked it away to forget.

That evening Monty Ferret rode Ladyhawke from the campfire into the open country, lost in memory.

CHAPTER 7

The driver had stopped, climbed down from the stagecoach to pick up the mail from the trail-box for Fort Laramie. One letter slipped from his glove, cartwheeled away in the wind. Before he could catch it, the snow-flash envelope fluttered at the hooves of the skittish creatures hitched to the Rock Springs–Denver *Comet*.

Rondo, the lead delphin, whinnied and reared from the flash, then he bolted and the animals ran for their lives. The stagecoach leaped away, driverless, pounding down the narrow desert trail, sagebrush blurring by, the six runaway delphins not pulling the comet so much as frantic to get out of its way.

The clank and jangle of the harness disappeared in a storm of high wheels spinning, iron rims crashing through sand and rock, the coach tilting, swerving.

Tumbled from the velveteen seat within, the beautiful Dulcimer Ferret gasped but did not cry out. Sole passenger, top-level courier for the governor of Wyoming Territory, she knew the West. Those delphins were far more frightened than she, and they'd drag a capsized coach nonstop, drag it to a trail of kindling in the desert.

She leaped for the hatch overhead, forced it open, fought to climb through and catch the reins loose-tied at the driver's seat.

The coach flew over a rise, crashed to earth in a cloud of spraying rock and dust, a snap of breaking springs, Dulcimer slammed from the hatch against the wooden armrest to the tilting floor.

At once she was on her paws, blood streaming from a gash on her head, the coach careening downhill toward the edge at Laramie Rim.

She threw herself again at the hatch, this time struggled through, caught the seat midjounce with one paw, grabbed the bundle of reins with the other, pulled hard.

Paws braced on the topping-rail, she strained against the tall brake handle, smoke streamed from the wheels. Still the delphins galloped for the cliffs, uncaring, desperate to escape the coach.

Mindless of disaster ahead, Dulcimer Ferret snapped the reins an expert turn around the gully-head, hauled back with all her might.

"There we go," she cried, the coach thundering, crashing on. "It's all right, you delphins, everything's all right!"

Heads high against the tension bar-tight on their reins, hooves sliding against the weight behind them, hearing her voice soothing, calling, the delphins slowed, ever so slightly, cliffs stark and close.

"Whoa down, now! Whoa down, little ones."

Gallop to canter went the delphin team, then trot to walk and finally to stand, sides heaving, heads turning toward the driver as Dulcimer eased the reins.

The lovely ferret slipped from the high seat, ran at once to the lead delphin, held his neck, stroked his nose. The cliff dropped sheer, less than a hundred paws distant.

"There now, there's my good delph. We had a nice run, didn't we?"

She ruffled the satin mane, softly, as though time had stopped. In a moment it did.

"CUT! And print! Spectacular shot, Jasmine!" Gemini Ferret released the bullhorn trigger. He looked to the camera operator perched behind the eyepiece, location baseball cap turned backward, embroidered silver on black, sweeping letters: *Dulcimer Ferret.*

The C.O. nodded. "Got it, G.F."

The director trembled, deep to his bones. He lifted the bullhorn once more. *"Terrifying, Jasmine,"* he called to his leading lady, *"but spectacular!"*

He didn't care if his star had grown up a ranchkit in Montana, he didn't care she was an expert rider. That shot was too close to the edge for Jasmine Ferret, megafilm or not.

"We won't need to cover that, will we, Streak?"

"No, sir. It's safe."

The director glanced at the clock, squinted to the angle of the sun. "A break, gentleferrets, then let's set scene ninety-one."

In the desert by the stagecoach, Montgomery Ferret shrugged out of his hidden harness on the down-camera side of the lead delphin and grinned at the actress.

"You had me goin', Cheyenne. Another second or so, I was about to ask Rondo to haul up pretty short." He patted the lead delphin, offered a carrot-cube the animal quickly accepted.

Jasmine smiled back. "Another second or so, Monty, I'd have been hoping you would!" She touched the syrup blood with her paw. "Am I a mess?"

"You could never be that, Cheye. I swear, the world's the richer for getting to watch you on-screen!"

She touched his shoulder. "Thanks for being here, Monty. I wouldn't have done the film without you to back me up."

The ranchpaw nodded. "You're doing fine, kit, I haven't had to step in once. But I'm happy to ride around and watch."

All the fame, he thought, and she hasn't changed. Not toward me, nor anybody. She's still the kit next door, loves the movies.

The script ferret approached, delicate, courteous. "We're setting up for ninety-one, Miss Jasmine. Makeup is going to want you to stop by, when you can . . ."

"You mean they want me right now, don't you, Jessie?"

A quick smile. "Sooner's probably better than later, Miss Jasmine."

"On my way." But she tarried.

"Monty . . ."

"Yes, ma'am."

"I know we wanted our dinner tonight . . ."

Monty gathered the tangled reins, fastened them neatly at the topping-rail, "That's no problem, Cheye. You've got to be tired, this close to wrap. We'll have it some other time."

"Oh, no! I mean, could we meet earlier? We've been so rushed, we haven't talked, there's so much to say."

There was no hiding his pleasure. "You name the minute."

"After the dailies this evening, come by my trailer. We'll have our dinner in, if you want, a little more time to talk."

"You don't need to rest?"

"You are my rest, Monty." Then she turned and hurried off to makeup.

The burly ranchpaw felt like a kit again, slipping out his window to ride in the moonlight with his friend.

Monty turned away, back to the team of stunt delphins.

"That was a good job, guys and gals." More carrot-cubes appeared for all, and from the hackamore at Rondo's muzzle he led them, a slow walk, back to the trail. "You are a team of one-take delphins, if ever there was. You are professionals." He winked at the leader. "And you did have me goin', Rondo. That was right down to the edge."

The delphin nodded, satisfied. But then he nudged the wrangler, as much as to change the subject, *Does that sound right to you, Monty, that my character would bolt and run away from a letter blowing in the wind? The script says it's supposed to look like a bat. Couldn't we have a real bat, a big one? Then I agree, my character would bolt!*

Monty smiled. "We don't write the script, Rondo. We just make it come alive."

The delphin sighed. *All the same, between you and me . . .*

"Between you and me? A big white bat coming at me, I'd be a lot more likely to bolt than he drops a letter . . ."

"Monty," came the voice of the assistant director on the bullhorn, "would you check the coach, please? We'll need another shot if we can, Lyndelle doubles for Jasmine, this time the close shot on the delphins, and we don't need to take it so near the Rim."

Monty called back. "Coach is fine, sir." Special-built, steel-reinforced, it could take ten runaways between repairs.

"Ready for close-ups, Rondo, everybody! Thirty minutes!"

The silence of agreement.

"All right," said Monty, "let's bring her back up on the road."

The delphins clambered up the loose-rock slope at the edge of the trail, empty stage clattering behind.

A few steps, and the leader nudged Monty once more.

"What's on your mind, Rondo?"

The delphin tossed his head, *If you get a chance, could you talk to G.F.? Tell him about the bat? I'm sure he'd agree: a big white bat, a delphin-eater. Else he's going to lose the audience—"What kind of delphin runs away, somebody drops a letter?"*

Monty patted the animal. "I just work here, same as you, Rondo," he said, "but I'll ask."

Later, stroking his black whiskers, Gemini Ferret listened to Monty, nodded. A fine idea. Your delphin's right. That's the better shot.

In the final cut of *Dulcimer Ferret,* the letter dropped, it blew in the wind, billowed into a death-color bat near the size of Rondo himself. Test audiences were hypnotized by Jasmine Ferret, but when asked about the runaway scene, not a single viewer blamed the delphins for bolting.

Monty looked at her in the candlelight, the rush and dust of the day settled and gone. She wore a sheer sky scarf and a locket: a silver heart.

"You ought to know I'm happy for you, Cheyenne," he said at last. "You're good at this business. I'm proud of you."

"Thanks, Monty." She smiled at the strong steadfast ferret her young riding teacher had become. "We have a good script, don't we?"

He looked at her, level dark eyes. "It's not the script. Do you know they cried, the crew, watching the dailies yesterday? They watched you on the screen and they had tears in their eyes. I'm talking about the *crew*!"

"Monty, I'm doing what I dreamed I could do. It's hard, sometimes. There's a price, but . . ."

She fell quiet, shifted her talk to telepathy and knew he could understand her wordless, how she felt, what she missed.

He missed it too, and knowing her sad beyond his means to comfort, he spoke again. "Pretty locket."

She brushed a tear, thanked him silently for changing the mood. "Want to see?" She slipped it from her neck, placed it before him.

"I'd best not."

"Oh, go ahead, ranchpaw. It won't bite you. Open it."

He touched the clasp and the silver heart sprang open. Inside, a single blue mountain daisy. He blinked, looked at her. "I remember."

That was dangerous, too. She turned the talk yet again.

"CineMustelid?"

"Still there in Little Paw," he said. "Alexopoulos doesn't brag about you, but he lets it be known that Jasmine Ferret sold tickets from this very booth, and she sat in this seat, and that one, and that one . . . He loves you, Cheye."

"I love him, too. I owe him."

Meals barely touched, they talked that evening about the days when they were kits together, the rides they took, she yearning to know that Sable Canyon was safe, their secret meadows, their old friends.

"Tell me, Monty. The most important event for you since . . . since we were together."

That would have to be his wild delphin encounter, what they did at the pond when they found the ferret was not just listening, he was understanding most of what they said.

"That big guy!" Monty shook his head. "Cheyenne, after all my guessing, clue by clue, I knew their language. It's not words, it's . . . I had followed them all the way to Button Water, up the draw from Johnny Polecat's old cabin, and the Alpha, the leader, I watched him say to the others, *Our ferret friend thinks he knows what we're saying!*"

Monty took a sip of mountain-water from the glass in front of him. "Then he angled to my left, as if I were a delphin myself, and he said, *If this kit can understand me, he'll wade out till his nose is just above water. And if he does that, we'll show him what no ferret has ever seen. I want you all to form a circle around the edge, and then real slowly, every one of us, we'll bow to him. But nobody move yet, he's got to wade in the water to his nose.*"

Monty's eyes were bright, remembering. "Now this is a bond of twenty-four wild delphins, Cheyenne, they're going to make a circle and they're going to bow to me! I watched the Alpha say that." He stopped, tried again to explain. "It's not words, they use. It's not even sounds, all the time. It's little movements, they shift their weight, shake their mane, flick an ear or an eyelash. And it's in their minds. There's nothing they can't say!"

She watched her old friend, the story gentled in his love for the animals.

"If I walked into the pond, now, they were all to circle and bow. So I showed 'em. I walked straight out into that water." He laughed at himself. "Mind, it was springtime, the snow melting. But I was so excited, Cheye, I can't tell you. I was going to say I understood! So out into that . . . well, it was liquid ice. I walked until just my nose was above the water,

nose and whiskers and my eyes, I was willing to freeze to death, looking for what they were going to do. And do you know what they did, do you know what those delphins did?"

"They spread out around the pond," she said, charmed by his tale, "left and right, and they formed a circle . . ."

He shook his head, a grin to melt her heart. "Nothing! They did *nothing*! They looked at me as though I was gone crazy, some ferret fell into the pond!"

"Not even one little bow?"

"Oh! that was a cold ride home! They were whinnying and laughing, behind me."

"Monty! That was cruel of them!"

He held up a paw in the delphins' defense. "They didn't push me, Cheye. They didn't force me. You've got to love an animal's got a sense of humor." He touched his glass, too happy to drink. "Next time I found them, the Alpha came over and he said he was sorry for their little joke, that I nearly froze. But his ears were way forward and his nose was twitching, the way they do when they laugh."

He went on for a while about the delphins. Never did he tell her that he had framed the photograph she had sent from the Young Actors' Home, that he kept it on the rough wooden desk of his cabin, that he talked to her picture every day, that he loved her still.

He told his stories and he listened to hers, about her first days in a strange city, jammed with auditions, with disappointment, triumph, with acting classes. About her discovery as an actress, in spite of her comment when the floodlight fell. The screen test for *First Light,* the leading role, how lucky she had been . . .

"Not lucky, Cheyenne," he said.

"There are lots of kits in Hollywood, Monty. Looking for a break. Not many of them ever . . . there's a lot of support, but it's really hard . . ."

He lifted his water glass, watched her in a quiet toast over the rim. "'*She's magic in the camera!*' Gemini Ferret said that, yesterday. He said everybody knows it: Jasmine Ferret's one of the greatest stars in the history of film. '*She's not her character, Monty, she's the soul of her character!*'"

"He said that?"

Monty nodded.

"How . . ." She reached for her glass. "How very kind . . ." Then she turned the conversation back to Montana. "Trish and Zander?"

He smiled. "Zander's in Scotland."

"Scotland!"

"So much I haven't told you. Zander cloned what they call Rainbow sheep. There's thousands of them now, they all want to see the Wild West. I'll be working with him, a little, on that. And Trish found her mate, she's married, moved to West Palm Beach, plays her harp still, recitals. Nakayama Ferret's a CPA, his own accounting firm."

"Trish loved her music and her numbers."

"So does Nakayama. He plays the flute, they do quadratic equations, for fun." Monty ran his paw over his forehead. "I'm an uncle, Cheye! Little Chloe. As cute a kit as you ever did see . . ."

His voice trailed off, lost in how swiftly the old days had passed. He hadn't known so many choices had gone by till this moment with his friend.

"And Monty?" she said.

He paused, decided not to burden her with his feelings. "Monty's doing fine. I'll probably never see the sights, like you and Zander and Trish. Don't really much want to. I'm happy in Montana. That's my home, Cheyenne. Montana and the delphins, ranchkits come learn to be 'paws. Pretty soon a fair-size flock of sheep coming to visit. I guess I love animals." He wondered, do I sound like a failure, explaining?

He knows himself, she thought. What a success he's become! She smiled, shy. "Is there somebody in your life?"

She thought he hadn't heard, her friend studying his water glass. Then he raised his eyes, looked directly into hers. "Why, yes, Cheyenne. There is somebody in my life."

She pushed his meaning away. "That's good to hear. I'm happy for you, Monty."

"Thank you. I hope there's somebody in your life, too."

Since she had become the world's Jasmine Ferret, since her first role in *The Lady Speaks,* the match-loving tabloid press had pondered who should be her mate. Her name had appeared a dozen times in the "Wouldn't It Be Nice?" column of *Celebrity Ferrets Today,* linked with Heshsty, with most of her leading actors. Once there had been rumors of Jasmine and Stilton Ferret, when she and the billionaire had passed through Los Angeles International Airport on the same day.

She thought about his question, wondered how to answer. "There is someone," she said.

"If you have any trouble with this animal," said Monty, "you tell him you've got a friend back home, he's a wild ferret and he fancies he's looking out for Cheyenne."

"You don't want to believe the press too much," she said. "The tabs mean well, but how they carry on! Heshsty's a dear, he's my pal, we love to work together. I'd like you to meet him, someday." She sighed. "No, the somebody I care about, I don't have any trouble with him, Monty." A trace of sorrow in her voice.

And there they left it. The hours weren't enough for what they needed to say, but neither would the day have been enough, or the week. Meal finished, candle burned low, Monty rose. "It's late. I'd best be on my way."

They stepped from her trailer into the cool air, her silver fur turned bright as snow in the moonlight. "You're glad, too, Monty? You're happy being a ranchpaw?"

He smiled. "I get kidded sometimes, I don't mind. I like being the ferret who talks to delphins, I like being a sheep-whisperer. There's a lot to learn that nobody knows, or probably much cares. I care. That's enough."

"I care, too." She hugged him gently, kissed his cheek the way she had when they had parted in Little Paw, so long ago.

They stood close in the quiet. If I tell her how I feel, he thought, and if she told me the same, what of her career? I'll not say a word to change her future.

"Well," he said, finally. "G'night, Cheyenne. You don't know how much . . ."

"I know." She leaned her head against his shoulder. If she told him how she felt, and if he felt the same, might it turn his destiny, might it stop a gift he would otherwise give to the world? She watched him for the longest seconds, considering. "I miss you, Monty. I miss home."

"I miss you too, Cheye. Someday maybe you'll come home. Not now. Not for a while. But . . ."

She warmed in his reminder that she had a choice. "Sometimes I forget I have a home. But I love my work."

He said nothing.

At last she let him go. "Night, Monty. Thanks. So much . . ."
She returned to the trailer, forced herself not to look
back. She so missed him, the quality of him, his confi-
dence. She missed the home she saw, shimmering there in
the window of her friend. Had Montgomery Ferret lifted
a paw or said a word, she would have stayed with him for
the rest of her life.

He did not. Quietly, the door between them closed.

Shooting on *Dulcimer* wrapped the next day. A chartered
helicopter arrived for Jasmine, she was off to the starring
role in *West from Home,* Taminder Ferret's towering
novel of a single-minded independent animal, her beauty,
her determination, her rise to stardom. Heshsty Ferret had
chosen her for the role, the tabloids would suggest, for the
pleasure of fiction become fact, scenes a mirror of the
movie star's life.

For Monty, it was that sudden. Coaxing delphins into
trailers, he glanced to watch the rotorcraft hovering down,
glanced again to see it lift off a few minutes later, tilt forward and disappear to the east. He didn't know it had
come for Jasmine till the A.D. mentioned she was gone.

CHAPTER 8

"Monty Ferret's Rainbow Sheep Resort and Ranchpaw Training Center, this is Sophia how may I help you?"

Jupe Ferret shook his head. Telephones, he thought.

He didn't spend much time in the office; came now in need of notepads for his saga. Why a ranch needs an office, or a telephone, he wasn't sure. Though the ranchpaw allowed that the world had changed since he and Monty were kits in bandannas and hand-me-down Western hats, one doesn't require a telephone in the high country to get along.

He listened with half an ear while the bright young office manager explained what he had heard more than once: We're sorry, but Rainbow wool may not be purchased outright. The sheep have the right of approval over every use of their product. Approval will not be granted without a meeting between the designer and the Rainbows themselves. The schedule is not difficult but the travel may be; our nearest airport is Helena, Montana, and the drive to the ranch will take nearly two hours. Thank you for calling . . .

The ranchpaw searched through the supply cabinets, found the clothbound tablets, wrote an IOU: *Two of these. Jupe.*

An automobile arrived outside, and shortly a knock on the counter, an executive inquiring. "Is this the office?"

"Yes, ma'am," said Sophia, rising to help, "you've come to the right place."

The telephone rang again. "Could you get that, Jupe?" the receptionist asked, sweetly.

Nearly to the door, holding his notebooks, the ranchpaw stepped back inside. He reached over the counter between a pair of city plants that would have been in real trouble if ever they had to live on the range, lifted the receiver.

"Sheep farm."

A soft French accent. "This is Monty Ferret's Rainbow Sheep Resort?"

"Yep."

"Last week I called. Could you tell me, now, a time to visit?"

"Friday," said Jupe. The day of the Canyon Performance, they'd be all brushed up.

"For approval? We can meet . . . ?"

"Yep."

"At . . . ah . . . three o'clock?"

"Yep."

"My name is"—the caller paused, understanding—"not necessary, is it?"

"Nope."

"Friday at three."

A crisp nod from Jupe, and he hung up the receiver. Then he left the office, headed toward the barn.

CHAPTER 9

Budgeron Ferret was up early, out in the predawn frost of the empty corral, writing pad on the middle rail, words by moonlight.

I'm scared, he wrote. *Tomorrow's the big ride, we're on our own, all the way to the high range, Thunder Mountain. Rainbows don't care, for them it's a picnic.* He paused, chewed on the end of his pencil. *Scares me most are the cliffs. Me and Strobe, we've got to keep them away from the edges. Cookie tells me be careful, there's places the trail's hard to find. Boa and Alla right behind us, don't let me lose the way. . . .*

There was a sound, the scrape of a match behind him in the barn, so sudden in the stillness that he spun around, dropped his pencil.

"Up early, Budgeron." Monty Ferret's mask and whiskers glowed in the light of flame touching lantern wick, sunrise not a hint in the east. He held the match upright, flicked the stem of it so quickly that the fire disappeared, held it for a while to cool, stuck it into his hatband.

"Yes, sir." Budgie stooped to recover his pencil.

The sheep-whisperer hung the lantern from a spike in the barn wall, leaned against the top rail of the corral, looked toward the mountain's ghost in the moonlight, nearly to the horizon. "Tomorrow's the big one."

"Yes, sir."

"Worried about the cliffs?"

"Yes, sir, I am."

"Good."

Budgie thought about that.

"It's the dangers you don't worry about that'll get you." Monty touched the wood of the rail. "When you're surprised, you're in trouble."

Then he turned, lifted the lamp, walked toward the ranch house. "Different from writing, I'll bet."

The ranchkit followed. "I wouldn't know, sir."

"You will." They walked in silence for a while. "The kits that come here, Budgeron, I can tell the ones going to change the world."

After a while Budgie found the courage to ask. "How do you tell that, sir?"

"They're the ones who know what they want." Monty ambled toward the dining hall, no hurry, lantern casting a sphere of golden light about the two animals. "You take Boa, he's brought his tool bag to a ranchpaw summer. No question that kit's going to be some master mechanic, one day. I don't know what kind of machine, but Boa's your animal makes engines run. Lives are going to depend on that kit, someday."

"So why is he here, sir? You don't need engines on a sheep ranch."

"Don't need writers, either." Monty opened the door to the building, washing in the first glow of sunrise. "Boa's here the same reason you are."

Budgie looked up, confident. "To prove we can do it."

The rancher led the way to a private wing of the dining hall, arches facing west, tiled path terminating in the white stucco of a walled patio: green plants potted close, a table, chairs, an adobe fireplace, coals sending a blanket of warmth near the table.

Monty pulled a chair out for Budgeron, seated himself opposite, set the lantern on the floor.

"You ever read Taminder Ferret?" he asked. *"Sea and Stars?"*

Budgie opened his mouth, closed it. *"Sea and Stars,* yes, sir! How did you know? *Winter Fire!* And *West from Home!* Those books, sir, he showed me what can happen! It stops being a page of print, the words they melt and they change into colors, into places, into animals, there's this *adventure,* sir, that the world disappears clear till the end and you're *gone,* and finally you wake up and somehow . . . somehow *all this came out of a book,* a book that you can hold in your paws but if you open it anywhere you're all tumbled back again into his world and *he's the only one can take you there!"*

It was more than he had said in one burst all summer.

The rancher listened, watched. "Want to talk about writing?"

Sunrise finally balanced on the hills toward Devil's Fork, Cookie appeared, rolling a polished wooden cart of ingredients before him. This morning he was respectfully silent, save for a subtle wink of recognition to Monty's guest. On the dining-hall blackboard, under *Monty's Private Breakfast This Morning With:* he had chalked *Budgeron Ferret.*

On the coolest spot of the grill he set his copper omelet pan, frothed and spiced *oeufs à l'orange* cooked slow and paper-thin, then deftly rolled for the two, the kit talking earnestly, the rancher listening, nodding now and then. Meanwhile, paws like an illusionist's, Cookie prepared *riz espagnol flambé* to half-circle the omelet, a splash of watercress, a meteor of Montana salsa. The meal he set before the two was lighter than morning air, wafting the colors of the day beginning.

"Thank you, Cookie," said Monty.

"Very much," said the kit. It felt odd to Budgeron, that today he was special, for once he couldn't chat and laugh with Cookie over the morning's exotic entrée.

The chef nodded to them both, a quiet smile, rolled his cart softly away, leaving coals simmering to themselves behind him.

The two talked on, until the ranch stirred awake an hour later to the enchanted clang of Cookie's triangle.

Monty rose. "I guess you've got a day ahead of you."

"Yes, sir. Thank you for your time and the breakfast!"

The kit was a few steps down the hallway when the rancher called after him, "Oh, Budgeron! For you."

Budgie turned back, blinked at Monty, holding out a book. "It's yours. It's for you."

"Thank you, sir!"

It wasn't till he was back in the bunkhouse, the others gone to breakfast, that he examined the gift.

White letters angling on a night-blue jacket: *West from Home.* The ranchkit opened the cover, his paws trembling. Opposite the title page, an inscription:

Whoever you are, young writer, bold dark sweeps of the pen, *Now that Monty Ferret has given this book to you, my torch is yours to light with your own flame, and one day to pass along.*

It was signed in a flourish: *Taminder Ferret.*

CHAPTER 10

Jasmine Ferret sat erect on the ruffles of her dressing-table chair, refused to be exhausted. Tuesday she had wrapped on *Pheretima,* an extravagant shoot in Venezuela. Wednesday a jet to the south of France for the Boxxes Film Festival, Thursday another round of interviews with news and magazine ferrets, last night the College of Actors Awards, evening swiftly turned to morning, no chance to rest, today a flight with an old friend to his mystery destination.

She leaned toward her mirror, ran an ebony brush through her fur, lifting and turning, leaving it tousled behind in what the world had come to call the Jasmine Look. At the edge of the mirror, an old railroad ticket, punched with a hole in the shape of a heart. Adjoining, a snapshot of a handsome young ferret in bandanna and hat.

Two crystal cubes were placed at the rear of the dressing table, each mounted on a silver spire, inscriptions illegible in the mirror. In front of them, hastily set down, two Whiskers, streamlined ferret sculptures, each quite heavy and gold. Engraved on the first, *COAA Best Actress: Jasmine Ferret.* On the other, the evening's highest award. *Kits' Choice: Jasmine Ferret.*

From her armoire she chose a filmy scarf by Donatien Ferret, cobalt and foam silver, to match her locket. The touch of a discreetly monogrammed whisker-comb, the lightest dust of chalk, she was ready a few minutes early.

Her face had changed, but she hadn't noticed. There was wisdom now, with the luminous beauty.

By the mirror a great round window framed her Malibu beachfront, ocean stretching beyond. Stark and sharp, that horizon. Not since she was a kit had she lived with the green fields and mountains of Montana. She missed the sound of the river, she missed still clear air.

She reached to the locket, opened it, watched an old scene conjure itself once more from that high mountain daisy, caught in time. She had been called to the stage, and she did not regret it. The price, though, the price! To live alone is to live without intimacy, a price that can turn one to stone.

I miss home, she thought, I miss it so much. And now . . . do I even have a home, anymore?

A soft knock. "Monsieur Donatien Ferret to see you, ma'am."

"Thank you, Gweneth." Jasmine did not bother to glance at the delicate clock on her dresser, for it would be precisely 1 P.M. The designer had a sense of business unsurpassed in the industry, and that sense began with punctuality.

The actress rose, followed the balcony of her dressing room to a sunlit living space, glass and polished wood and silk velvets, overlooking the sea.

A cosmopolitan animal, perfectly groomed, turned at her entry, a sand-color gift box near him on the table. His soft French accent: "Hallo, Jasmine. Congratulations once more. First your Ice-Cubes from Boxxes, last night Whiskers twice over! *Magnifique,* as always."

"Hello, Donatien. Thank you."

"This is not the best time? You're a little tired, a little sad."

The actress smiled. "I was, a while ago. You brighten my day."

"It is my happy spirit which does this for you. You have changes coming, Jasmine?"

One goes nowhere in business, Jasmine thought, without being sensitive to others.

"I'll tell you later." She noticed the box on the table, did not inquire.

"You promised to come with me, no questions," he said. "But a later day will also be fine . . ."

Jasmine smiled, shrugged away fatigue. "No questions. When do we leave?"

"Now." The designer lifted the gift box. "For you."

"Thank you. You're so kind." She untied the ribbon, lifted the lid. Within, under a veil of tissue paper, a wide-brim Western hat. Not a hat that a ranchpaw would wear, for it was blue, the color of Montana sky.

She looked up, startled, eyes wide to Donatien. *How could you know?*

As she seemed stunned at the sight, her friend lifted the hat from its box, set it back on her head. "Tsk," he murmured. He shook his head no, reset the hat, tilting it low over her eyes. He brightened. *"Voilà! C'est parfait!* Jasmine, not a word."

He turned her to the mirror, saw the look in her eyes. "Not a word! I know! *You love it!*"

☺

The two arrived at the Van Nuys airport, the actress and the designer, that glamorous pair from the white limousine, up the stairs of a business jet, *Donatien* lettered on its fuselage, gold against black. No one knew what Jasmine thought, dozing through the flight, the dust-blue Western hat pulled to shade her eyes, although a glimpse of the two would be reported next day in *Who's Together?* magazine.

They landed that afternoon at Helena Municipal Airport, stepped into a dark limousine and set off southward.

Jasmine listened as they drove, the designer stitching in a fabric of coincidence the depth of which he did not know.

For his new scarfwear, Donatien told her, he needed Rainbow wool and none other, and do you believe that in only one place can it be found? Calls to Montana, an appointment made for a touch of business, a minute for the canny Rainbows to agree that a line of haute-couture scarves in such exquisite taste was proper use of those rare colors.

The perfect day, he told her—Jasmine to join him for a rest, a grounding she could not help but enjoy, a visit to the hills and plains of which she had so often spoken, not far from her kithood home.

She nodded, a smile for her friend. "You're an angel, Donatien!"

He could not have known, nor did she wish to tell him just now. If such loving coincidence brought her here, would it not find Monty home, could their paths touch again?

She felt her heart beating. There's order in the world, she thought, there's a beautiful order in the world.

CHAPTER 11

Monty Ferret had ridden Ladyhawke the back way, following the streambed to Northstar, a town that now, with the success of the sheep resort, called itself Gateway to the Rainbows. By the road stood a sign painted by kits, depicting a countryside amok with fluffy colors.

He rode slowly, watched the hillsides, listened to the stream, the birds, to his own heart speaking.

Everything I wanted, he thought, everything I hoped for, it's come true. I'm just a country ferret, loved my mountains, the outdoors, Montana, and here I live. I loved my delphins, wanted to understand all the animals around me, now I do, pretty well, and we all get along just fine. I wanted to make their dreams come true, the little Scots, and the ranchkits, too. He smiled. We show 'em Action, Adventure, Romance on the High Plains! and sure enough, the sheep are happy and the kits go home strong and wise and kind, they earn their own respect. That's what I wanted for them, and that's what I got.

I've had a few questions of my own, he thought, found a few answers that work for me.

He lifted his hat and ran a paw over his forehead, smoothing the fur. A soul can learn a lot, in one lifetime, but even so . . .

Ladyhawke huffed, stopped, blinked to watch a small ferret, appeared from empty air.

On the middle of the stream, a shimmering nutmeg coat, a clove-color mask, solemn amusement.

"Hello, Monty." The ferret's dark eyes locked on his. "Need some help?"

The rancher smiled down at her, nodded at the current splashing over her paws. "Counts as pawprints, does it?"

"It does, thank you," she said. "Need some help?"

"I miss her, Kinnie. I miss Cheyenne."

"She's—"

"I know she's got her destiny, I know I've got mine. I ask within, and the answer comes back that everything's okay, it's just the way we meant it to be. I've done mostly what I came here to do, seems to me. Maybe she has, too, maybe not. But when I ask why did we want to be born in Little Paw, why did we become such good friends if all we were going to do was part forever"—he touched his hat lower— "what I get is *there's a reason,* and I'm not sure that's what I want to hear."

"It won't be—"

"Is there something we have to do that we haven't done? You got some sort of cosmic agenda for us, Kinnie, or is this what it feels like, to know everything and still be sad? Missing her, that's a sign I'm not a finished philosopher ferret, I guess."

"Could be." The little animal took a small step upward, to the top of the wavelets. No more splashing about her ankles, no more pawprints in the water. "And it could be that missing her's a sign of another destiny between you. Could be a sign that you haven't done everything you came to do, after all."

"You can tell me what's going to happen, can't you?"

She shook her head. "Sorry. I can tell you a rule of space-time: *What's going to happen has already happened.* I can tell you a rule of consciousness: *What you perceive is up to you.*"

"And you're going to tell me I'm a fool, feeling sad when always and everywhere I'm surrounded by love?"

The dark eyes twinkled. "No. I'll let you say that yourself."

He smiled at her. "Did I ask you to come find me here, talk to me this way?"

As though she hadn't heard, Kinnie looked to the horizon, to Northstar Mountain. Then she turned back and nodded brightly. "You're a dear ferret, Monty. You've learned much. You are greatly loved."

Ladyhawke blinked at where her rider's other-level friend had stood, the stream chuckling over empty stones. The delphin tossed her head, *Wouldn't hurt to listen, Monty Ferret.*

I listen, Lady-H, he said to her in his mind. Takes me a while, sometimes, but I listen.

Delphin and rider came over the rise south of town, on a trail lifted from stream to pine needles underhoof, now and then a glimpse of buildings beyond the trees.

"Your big day, Monty!" The café door hadn't closed behind the rancher when Quill raised a glass of mountain-water, a toast. The other ferrets turned: "H'lo, Monty."

"Not my big day," he said, "it's theirs. Those sheep are good little hoof-dancers! Can't sit still, watching."

How hard they had practiced these last months, the Montana Rainbow Zouave Rhythm March Corps and Scottish Dance Company! Wandering off had dropped to zero, the sheep who chose not to audition for the Canyon Performance mesmerized by the rehearsals.

He sat at the counter, his back to Main Street.

"What's it to be, Montgomery?" Roxy Ferret never knew what Monty would order. It was always something different, unless he was feeling lonely.

"How about a fresh strawberry?"

"One fresh strawberry, comin' up," she said. I wouldn't be lonely, the proprietress thought, if I had all that excitement going on, the Canyon Performance tonight.

"Thank you, Rox."

"I sense you feel down a little, kit," she said, serving the fruit sliced in four.

"Oh, no. I got nothin' to feel down about."

At that moment a black limousine passed the café, shadowy figures within. Roxy grinned. "There's another one!"

By the time Monty turned to see, the vehicle had disappeared, faint trail of dust filtering down.

"We are on the map, kits," said Roxy. "I can't guess how many of those, lately. Two dozen if there was one. All up to your ranch."

"They like the wool," said Monty. "Can't say as I blame 'em. It's like nothin' you've seen, is it?"

"Pricey," said Quill, "but I've got to admit it is plumb beautiful."

"Got to admit," said Monty, softly.

Jasmine Ferret, suggested Donatien go alone to his meeting with the Rainbows, but the designer would have none of it.

"They are beautiful," he said. "How often does one get the chance to meet such creatures? Please come."

So Jasmine went along, quietly.

It did not go as well as Donatien had hoped. The Rainbows were distracted, the Canyon Performance just hours away, the sheep uneasy in the presence of the fashion designer. Would he find their dance boring, would he judge them harshly? The more they thought, the more the little sheep felt that it would be best not to approve a sale to Donatien Ferret. Not today.

The designer felt the animals' hesitation, discomfort. "These scarves. I've designed them so the colors themselves warm and protect."

The Rainbows looked at one another. Not today.

Jasmine rose from her place at the edge of the room. Monty had told her long ago, "Ever you find an animal you don't understand, ask yourself, *What's it thinking?*"

What were they thinking now, the Rainbows?

From old practice she sensed her way into their thought, a display of mind and spirit unanimous, for the moment, in discomfort.

Donatien is a designer, yes, the sheep were worrying, but he is a showferret as well. What if he doesn't like our performance? What then? Will he not care so much for who we are, and for our wool, and will his work not be so beautiful as it must be?

Wordless, Jasmine glided along their level of thought, a place of broad views and wide verandas. The Rainbows looked at each other. The only one who had met them here was Monty Ferret. Now this one.

In her mind, Jasmine suggested a solution. What if with every scarf might come a card telling the background of the rare sheep, photos of the Rainbows in dance? With each a testament to the Montana Rainbow Zouave Rhythm March Corps and Scottish Dance Company? Could this make a difference, that they're more than wool, they're more than the most beautiful wool in the world?

Within, the climate of thought shifted. Donatien Ferret would recognize us as artists, too?

Jasmine nodded. If he did not respect you, he would not have come.

And the card, would it be in color?

Yes.

Thank you. And a decision: Done.

The Rainbows, sensitive creatures, once ready to file from the room in a cloud of foreboding, now trotted to the written request, stamped it *Approved,* little hoofprints. And would Donatien care to join them, last rehearsal before the show?

He would be honored.

Respect and understanding go a long way, in business.

Jasmine walked alone from the conference room, across the grass by the dining hall, toward the office. Alone. Jasmine Ferret the actress, she thought. So much recognition, so much isolation. So much of life alone!

But this was delicious Montana. She sniffed the mountains in the air, the forests and streams, she sniffed her past, the kit Cheyenne from Little Paw. She touched the locket on its chain around her neck, lost in thought.

"Jasmine Ferret?"

She stopped, turned at a familiar voice. By the door to the dining hall, copper pot in one paw, chef's hat askew, stood Gerhardt-Grenoble Ferret.

"Gren?" This was not possible.

The silver ferret ran to embrace her friend, his copper pot a-clang to the ground. "Gren, what happened to you? You disappeared! Armond . . . not a word, said he'd promised not to tell!"

Her fatigue vanished in discovery. "This is Montana!" she said. "This is my home! What are you doing . . ." She stood back and took in the sight of him.

"It's my home, too, Jasmine. No more Grenoble. Call me *Cookie.*"

"Cookie!" She laughed. "But you were happy at La Mer!"

The chef looked toward the office, took Jasmine's paw and led her to the kitchen. Simple woodstoves, wooden counters, bowls and pans, utensils made by paw. About them, the room bustled quietly, Bud and his assistants preparing the chuckwagon buffet for evening concertgoers.

"I was happy, for a long time, the challenge. But after you're the best, after you're Number One, then what? I was the star, I was giving interviews, or I was traveling, some hotel room, alone. What kind of life is that, alone? There is a challenge beyond Number One."

"I didn't know, Gr—Cookie."

"You know. For that is your life, too."

He reached overhead, brought down a giant wooden salad-bowl, set a dish of butter lettuce leaves in front of her on the counter, took cold-pressed virgin olive oil from the cupboard, and a bottle of balsamic vinegar, large bottles, labels in Italian. How can I get through to her?

"Wash your paws, and dry," he said. "Tear the leaves into little pieces, please. Small little pieces."

Silent, watching her friend in control of his world without a word spoken, Jasmine felt a peace about him that she had not noticed before.

"Oh you, Jasmine Ferret." He laughed. "You know what kind of life that is! No secrets from Cookie! I was Celebrity

Chef, all my friends the celebrities, too . . .*Jasmine Ferret's* my friend, her picture with me, signed, on the wall at La Mer! But she didn't know: Gerhardt-Grenoble's alone! And why should she care?" He smiled, shrugged. "That's no kind of life."

She tore the lettuce very small. "We missed you."

"That's no kind of life," he repeated. From beneath the spice rack he pulled a mortar and pestle fashioned out of rock from Northstar Mountain, placed a sprig of sage on the stone. "That is no life and you know it, Jasmine Ferret." He waved to the sky, the mountains west. *This! This is life!*"

"But you're alone, Cookie! What difference does it make, Beverly Hills or Manhattan or Northstar, Montana?"

The chef had been shaking his head all through her words.

"Not alone?" asked Jasmine.

He crushed the sage, chose and added two sprigs more, ground them together. "I was led to this place, Jasmine. Very first day, my reward, I met Adrienne. You will meet her."

"*Adrienne Ferret?* MusTelCo's CFO? She's here? When she left New York for the simple life, she came here?"

He nodded.

Guided by their highest right, she thought. "I'm . . . I'm happy for you, Cookie."

"When is Cookie going to be happy for you, Jasmine Ferret?"

"There's nobody who knows who I am. There are ferrets in the world who could love Jasmine, but I'm not . . ." Lettuce-leaves unfinished, she turned to him. "Nobody knows who I am."

"Cheyenne Ferret knows." She looked up to him, startled. Before she could answer, ask how he knew that name, the chef caught her paw. "Let me show you."

He led the actress up a narrow flight of stairs, pressed open a wooden door. Before them a hallway of dark Spanish tiles, walls of rough adobe painted white, wooden beams overhead.

"Where . . . ?"

"Monty's gone. You need to see."

"These are Monty's rooms? He's not here? Cookie, this is wrong! Take me back!"

The chef stopped. No ferret leads another where it does not wish to go.

"Jasmine, listen!"

She was still. No ferret refuses when a friend asks it to hear.

"You've been invited!"

"But Monty's—"

"You've been invited since the day you left Little Paw!"

Jasmine felt a wave of shock through her, from the tip of her tail to her soft brushed whiskers. "Gren—"

"I'm not Gerhardt-Grenoble! You're not Jasmine! Not here!" His tail thrashed left-right. "Let me show you."

Cookie swept his paw toward the next door in the hallway. Another few steps . . .

The room was silent, no one there. Caution overcome by curiosity, the actress moved ahead, poked her nose around the corner, stepped into the room.

Before her lay a place from her past, not a replica but the same loving air of home in Little Paw. An open fireplace, a wide couch, its wood frame built by paw, carved relief on the back: two kits in a meadow of mountain daisies. A hat rack made from a pine branch. It felt familiar, she couldn't place it.

On the wall, a photo of young Cheyenne Ferret astride her delphin, standing at the upper ford of the Big Paw, the glint of Hidden Lake through the trees in the background. She thought she had forgotten that photo.

She moved slowly through the room, taking it in. A red gingham picnic cloth draped from a peg on the wall, torn movie-ticket stubs: *Desperate Voy* . . . A photo unframed on the desk, taken not so long ago: the elderly Boffin and Starlet together at the corner of her parents' corral. Her paw went to the image, stroked it. A slow whisper: "My little Starlet . . ."

She did not turn to Cookie. "Would you mind if I stayed for a minute? Would Monty mind?"

"He has told me, Cheyenne," said the chef, from the doorway. "I don't know he has told anyone else. It is your place, here. Stay as long as you wish."

She didn't answer, nor meet his eyes. He closed the door.

Jasmine removed her hat, hung it gently on the branch of that familiar tree. My oldest friend, she thought. How far we've come from the days we were kits.

He had to stay in Montana, I had to go.

She curled into the couch, stared at the fireplace. *Unless I do my best, Monty, I'll never know.*

She had done her best. She had paid her price and she had made a difference. And now . . .

She closed her eyes. With Monty gone, in this place so much like home, for just a little while, she needed to rest.

☙

Montgomery Ferret arrived home not long before the Canyon Performance was to begin. He'd watch, he decided, from the bluff above the table rock that the Rainbows had chosen for their premiere, a stage closed on three sides by cliffs, a place of echoes.

Down the hallway, he noticed that the door to Cheyenne's room was closed.

He frowned. Who's been here? No one closes that door. Cookie?

The rancher touched the wood and it swung aside. The room was empty, seemed empty.

Monty's heart stopped. For there, from the pine branch he had brought down from Sable Canyon, hung a sky-blue Western hat.

CHAPTER 12

All the town was there, ferrets come in pickup trucks, in cars, on delphins. They rode up, hiked up the back trail to see the Rainbows' show, proud of their little Montana Scots.

The wide arc in front of the cliff was packed with concert-goers, the sun beginning to sink at the western side, toward the canyon top. High on the rim, near the edge, stood ten Scottish ferrets, five pipers, five drummers, in full-dress tartan caps and scarves. The pipers silently fingered the chanters of their instruments though they had played the

marches and reels a hundred times before. It's a big crowd, down there. Two minutes to go.

Hidden in the arroyo behind the bare rock stage were the Rainbows, all the little clones feeling the same butter-flies within, all moving through the march and dance routines high-speed in their collective mind. Along the steep hairpin road down the face of the cliff above the stage, a strange sight: four ranchpaw pickup trucks parked, front wheels blocked, rear axles lifted on jacks, the drivers there, waiting for the show.

The lead piper nodded to his mates, they huffed to inflate the bagpipes, the sound of drones began, frail for a moment, then all at once the chanters, a cry of eagles aloft. The crowd below went still, blood chilled in the skirl of the pipes and, long seconds later, the first beat of the drums.

The pipers' melody rang out, an ancient slow-march: "Scotland's Lambs Bid Dreams O' Flight." Slow it was, freighted with thrill tight under rein, the audience beginning to tremble.

Now another sound, though the stage remained bare—a slow stamp of hooves in unison. At last, up from behind the smooth rock, a movement, the peaks of one tam-o'-shanter, of five, of ten, of twenty, and now from each side, the Rainbow Zouaves streamed upon the stage.

Gradually did the melody of the pipes increase its tempo, faster came the march and stamp of hooves on rock, the sheep expressionless, colors brushed and matched in ranks. Some said later that it was the sound of steel hoof-taps they heard; others said no, hooves alone, but echoing like steel from that hard stage.

It was a grand start, the crowd scarcely breathing. Faster came the pipes, faster the march, hooves united thunder, then the first surprise syncopation, and the crowd burst in a cheer of uncontained delight.

Slow-time, full-time, double-time, skirled the pipes, quick-time, double-quick, triple-quick, till the storm of hooves was a giant engine spun by the Zouaves, their bright forms swaying, turning smoothly, their feet nearly invisible for the speed of the march and then in one breath, instant

Silence.

Echoes.

Echoes . . .

The crowd detonated, unable to hold its tension, a sound so sharp and affirm that several of the marchers, still breathing hard, blinked in the storm of it.

Thus began an evening that no one would forget. After the Zouave marchers came the Rainbow hoof-dancers, led at first by the pipes into wild complex rhythms and finally *a cappella,* hooves became their own hurricane melody. At one moment there were no fewer than four sheep air-borne at once, launched inverted from dashes up the vertical walls of the stage. At another, one could count six separate living pinwheels a-spin, fast enough the colors began to blend.

Sun fading, the show finished to a climax that brought nearly a hundred Rainbows onstage, Zouaves and dancers together, all bodies still, all hooves flashing, the sound, despite its intricate rhythm, nearly deafening.

Sitting easily astride Ladyhawke, Monty Ferret watched from the bluff, as swept in delight as any kit from town.

Show over, stage empty in the dusk, the crowd refused to leave, applause roared out unabated, cheers cried for more.

"What do you say, Cheye? Do our little guys have a future?"

There were tears in her eyes, the excitement of the show, she thought. "They're . . . they're fabulous, they're spectacular, they're five-star, Monty, they're ten-star. I'm all Hollywood and I don't want to be."

"Then maybe you could be Montana, instead."

She watched his eyes. He did not turn away, a level gaze, not kidding at all.

In the dark, then, over unceasing applause, radiance. The four ranchpaws on the road above pulled their pickup headlight switches together, and the stage illuminated. With the light, the pipes began again. *Encore!*

Monty nodded to Cheyenne, touched Ladyhawke's mane. Their two delphins moved down the bluff, away from the stage and the crowd, toward the high land north of the ranch.

"My guess is that we're going to have a moonrise here pretty soon, that it's going to be near full, right about yonder, up from Northstar Mountain."

He pointed. Already the mountain glowed, backlit in moonlight.

Cheyenne Ferret laughed. "Oh? 'It's going to appear right about yonder'?"

"Now you don't like my talk, do y'?" he said, eyes twinkling. "Y' don't care for m' idiom?"

She turned to him as they rode, side by side, into the night. "I love your idiom, Monty! I love your talk. It's just, I've just been so long in a place . . . where there is no yonder."

He did not reply.

"Is it time I took the train from Hollywood, Monty? One-way ticket home, no looking back?"

"Are you asking my opinion?" He lifted his hat, ran a paw over his forehead, smoothing the fur. "You do what you know is highest for you, Cheye. If you decide to take that train, I've got no problem with you looking back at all. I suspect, by the time you get here, you'll be looking forward again."

She nodded. Having climbed certain peaks, she thought, we descend no more, but spread our wings and fly beyond. "When I come home, Monty, do I get my yonder back?"

"You do."

She smiled happily, said nothing more.

They rode toward the slopes of Northstar Mountain, the two of them together, into the moonlight.